BOY AT THE WINDOW

BOY AT THE WINDOW

A Novel by OWEN DODSON

THE CHATHAM BOOKSELLER
CHATHAM, NEW JERSEY

Copyright 1951 by Owen Dodson.

All rights reserved, including the right to reproduce this book, or portions thereof, in any form.

Grateful acknowledgment is made to the copyright owners for permission to quote from the following songs.

The lines from Around the World with the Children *by F. B. Carpenter are used by permission of the publishers, the American Book Company*

"Yes! We Have No Bananas"
Copyright 1923 by Skidmore Music Co., Inc. Copyright renewed.

"The Master Went Alone to Pray"
Words by Priscilla Heath.

"In the Garden"
Copyright 1912, 1940 renewal. The Rodeheaver Company, owner. International copyright secured.

Designed by Maurice Serle Kaplan.

*Library of Congress No. 74-182682
ISBN 0-911860-10-X
Reissued 1972 by The Chatham Bookseller
By arrangement with Farrar, Straus and Giroux, Inc.*

For Peggy and Leonard Rieser

All characters depicted in
this book are imaginary.

". . . and he will be so as a boat baptized for a brave journey."

                                          SEBREE

BOY AT THE WINDOW

HE ran down the hall lickety-split as if a hard ball were chasing him or that mean old principal, Mr. Heindrick. Miss Raidin's voice shot at the back of his head like BB's, "Coin, Coin Foreman, come back this minute."

He wanted to stop. Maybe she could somehow wash the ink off his hands but could she get the whole mess of it out of his suit and his underwear and off his shoes . . . could she do that! Mama could and she wouldn't scold telling him he should be ashamed of himself, a great big nine-year-old boy and clumsy as a nanny goat. Anyway why did Miss Raidin have to send him after ink, he wasn't nobody's teacher's pet?

"Coin, Coin, Coin," the voice rang in his head like nickles.

A door ahead was opening, Miss Binatree's. As he darted past he heard her needle voice and Miss Raidin's too, faraway at room 107, singing in a duet with one word in the key of G like on the round harmonica Miss Van Epps used in music period.

"Coin, Coin, Coin."

He almost tripped going down the stairway clearly marked UP. If they caught him he'd have to slap chalk-dust out of erasers for a week . . . after school. Or maybe worse.

Outside in the sun he noticed that the ink had turned his brown hands the color of carbon paper under thin, shiny gloves of isinglass. They looked permanently disfigured. Running his hands over his knickers he felt the undried ink, became more excited, rushed down hot, empty, two o'clock Belmont Avenue, dodged a honking auto, turned into Berriman Street and bumped Davey Carth, in his starched white suit, right into the gutter. Like an agitated target, Davey squirmed and cried, brushing at his Eton collar, "Wait till I tell my mother on you, then you'll see."

"Aw," panted Coin.

"Whatdidyasay?"

"I don't chew my cabbage twice," Coin mocked and resumed the getaway toward his house. "It serves him just right. Let him tell his mother. I know about her."

Just two days ago, Wednesday, while he was playing sidewalk handball with his brother Woody and Abie Schneider, Mrs. Carth had called to give him a bag of peanuts which he accepted greedily. Mixed with them were two or three pieces of dried dog doo. As he threw the bag away in disgust Davey scrambled for them but was stopped by his laughing mother's "Davey!" She continued laughing like it was the biggest joke in the world. The inside of her mouth was the color of ripe bananas and between her teeth were brown, moss stripes. The kids didn't laugh though. They vowed that Davey wouldn't ever play with them again, not handball or ring-a-leavio or mumblety peg or anything else again. Woody solemnly spit on each peanut to make sure Davey wouldn't pick them up after they left. Woody had a good aim. Davey stood inside his gate and cried. Mrs. Carth stopped laughing long enough to say, "Come in the house, Daveyboy, before those rag-a-muffins hurt my little darling."

Woody sang after Davey, "Before those ragged muffins hurt my little darlinggggggggggggg."

Mrs. Schneider who had been watching from the next door clamped down her window with an "Oi, oi, joi, joi."

Coin knew about Mrs. Carth all right. And he wasn't ever going to collect horse manure for her back yard, not ever. He'd get a nickel somewhere else next Saturday.

Mrs. Carth's husband had died six years ago and since then how she got money was the mystery of the block.

All kinds of gossip hung around her house. Mrs. Schneider, who was an all-day-long porch sitter, said that the mailman never entered the Carth gate, so her money didn't come that way. Besides Mrs. Carth never went out except to shop at Feinstein's Blake Avenue Market. Mrs. Eurydice Jeffers clucked that she had known a woman in Panama who had money hidden away in all sorts of places. Even in the icebox.

"Oh, that Carth's smart all right."

"Nu? Oi, joi, joi," Mrs. Schneider always commented. The singsong voice said mystery knowledge.

How to get home without passing the Carth house was the problem. Coin knew that Davey was already there. He wouldn't mind the Carth scolding. It was the banana laugh that fascinated, scared and angered him. Laughter was mixed up with colors and fruits and smells. Now he was mad because Mrs. Carth's laughter was the yellow and brown of bananas. He liked bananas but hated her. When his Popa laughed there was a purple color, and a cigar smell. You laughed with Popa but always stopped short because in the first place you laughed even if you didn't understand the joke and you stopped because you realized you didn't; then too Popa could use the strap just as easily after laughing as before; so you never could tell. There was the cosy-snuggle-up laughter—Woody's was like that and no particular fruit was connected with it—only the color red and that was his favorite. Once, after he had gone to bed, he heard his mother laugh sweet pale blue. The next day he tried out all sorts of jokes and made up little funny stories to hear that color again but she only smiled.

As he neared Mrs. Carth's house, he noticed Davey scamper up the steps and enter the vestibule. He could almost smell Mrs. Carth's thick, yellow laughter even from two houses away. In front of Mrs. Schneider's he crossed his hands over the largest stain on his knickers and held his knees together to cover others. He was forced to walk knock-kneed. At her gate the laughing Mrs. Carth was a huge white duck and her arm a pointed wing, protecting Davey. That's just what she was—a duck—small head with the gray hair combed forward to bangs, flat chest, hips and behind humped out from her yellow and white gingham housedress. Davey called to Coin, "Whatsthematter, Coin, you got to go to the bathroom?"

Coin was infuriated. He forgot about inkstains and all. Letting a hand fly out to slap Davey, he felt his wrist in a rough vise, the Carth banana breath rush into his face. He shut his mouth tight and held his breath.

"Listen, you little dirty nigger, if you ever touch my Davey again, I'll throw you down the sewer. Look at his white suit. Get away from here or I'll sic the dog on you."

"Nigger, nigger," chanted Davey jumping up and down, "Dirty nigger."

Mrs. Schneider stopped rocking on her porch. "Oi, joi, joi, such a way to talk to the little kint, such a way."

Mrs. Carth whirled around, releasing Coin, and called, "You shut up, you lousy Jew, you." Grabbing

Davey by the collar she waddled up her porch and slammed the vestibule door.

Mrs. Schneider wailed, "In this neighborhood, such talk, such talk I never heard."

As he scooted across the street to his house, Coin felt something wild in his throat and his stomach expanded and contracted. In the lower hall of the tenement he just stood. The odor of that breath seemed part of his air even here. Automatically he waved his hands trying to fan away the smell or erase what he had heard. His wrist ached; his mind probed itself. Nigger. Dirty nigger. The word grew large like a balloon being blown up so big it filled the cracks and crevices in the hall, surrounded him. He tried to fight his way to an understanding. His hands peeled the word. Nigger. It meant nothing to him; but the way Mrs. Carth had said it, the way she had gripped his wrist, the way Davey had smirked, repeating his mother, the way Mrs. Schneider had chanted. He walked slowly to the back of the hall, down the familiar cellar steps, sought a dark corner and vomited up his lunch.

When Coin entered the dining room of the Foreman railroad flat there wasn't a sound except the clock pocking his senses.

"What is a nigger, what is a nigger?"

The question was answered by the clock.

"I don't know, ask your mother, I don't know, ask your mother, I don't know, ask your mother . . ."

All the oak furniture listened to Coin, everything heard, refusing to answer. No one was in the kitchen.

"Mama," he called softly. This was the first time in his life that she hadn't been home when he returned from school. The ticking followed him into the bedroom.

"I don't know, ask your mother, I don't know, ask your mother, I don . . ."

Sitting on what he and Woody called the low-down bed, because the legs were so short you could touch the floor and make patterns with your fingers before you went to sleep, he stared across at his parents' bed in the alcove. "Mama?" he whispered. The clock answered with the same refrain.

She must be somewhere in the neighborhood. She couldn't walk far, dragging her left leg and holding her left arm against her breast as if a pain were continually there to be soothed. "Mama?" Suddenly the house shook and a clanging noise slapped him. He rushed through the back parlor into the living room and stood at the window watching two hook and ladders zip by wobbling with a load of apparatus and men in bright-red helmets. School hadn't let out so only a few housewives stood on their porches. Mrs. Jeffers and Mrs. Schneider stopped talking. Mrs. Carth and Davey were at their gate. The laughter and smell returned, the word flew back into his mind and struggled there like the sparrow that had gotten caught in the mouse trap Popa had thrown into the back yard last year. "Those traps never did catch a thing," he commented. "It's highway robbery for stores to sell them."

Coin had always been excited by fires. Now he

simply pressed his pug nose against the window pane. Behind him the empty rooms were all ticking clock and no Mama; ahead identical, shabby, two story frame houses with porch, garden, fence and gate were faces, the opening doors, tongues, poked out making fun of him. Mrs. Carth must be the devil even Reverend Brooks feared and his mother, somewhere in the heat and smell of Brownsville, wasn't there to explain the word that had changed this solid street to the trembling one he saw through hot tears dropping on his hands. Out of the corner of one eye he saw his mother limping up the street. Even from half a block away she seemed larger than life size. With the sun making the edges of her body glow, he thought of statues in St. Gabriel's. He longed to hear the sweet blue laughter and feel her fingers pinching his cheeks. At breakneck speed he dashed through the house while the clock still ticked the same refrain, "I don't know, ask your mother, I don't know, ask your mother . . ."

"Set that bag in the kitchen, Coin, and then come here and tell me what's the matter. I won't scold about the ink because I know you didn't mean to do it. The Lord knows where you'll get another suit but we'll attend to that when Agnes comes home from school."

It took her a long time to take off her thin, patched coat. Coin stood on a chair and gently pulled her paralyzed arm away from the sleeve.

"Now tell me why that face is all smeared up with tears."

He nestled against her side and began tracing the wallpaper design on the other side of the room with his eyes. He couldn't get the words he wanted to say out properly. Mrs. Foreman pressed him to her. He trembled a little as he thought of the Carths, then said, "Mama, what's a nigger?"

"You go look it up in the dictionary."

"How do you spell it?"

"Why Coin, I thought you were smart."

"I can't spell that, never heard it before, Mama."

"According to the dictionary, that word signifies a bad person."

"Then I'm no nigger," Coin promptly answered.

"Of course you're not. Who said that word, son?"

"Mrs. Carth."

"Why? Something must have happened. Nobody talks like that on our street."

"Mrs. Carth and Davey do."

"What happened?"

"I bunked into Davey accidental and he fell down."

"I see."

"Mama, her teeth are so funny and . . . and she smells like bananas."

"Never mind her teeth and all that. And don't pay any attention to what she and Davey utter. Are you listening, Coin?"

"I'm glad I'm no nigger," he said abstractly.

"I brought you some candy." She took a caramel wrapped in cellophane from her apron pocket and handed it to him. "Now run along and play."

"What about my pants—the ink?"

She thought a moment. "We'll get Mr. Altar to dye them. You better wash your hands and face. Agnes will scrub them later on."

Suddenly Coin looked up at her calm face. "Laugh, Mama."

She only smiled, pinched his cheek and murmured, "Run along. Mrs. Quick will be here soon and we'll be busy, run along." He scampered into the bathroom.

Twice a week practical nurse, Mrs. Geneva Mason Quick, came hop-skip-jumping down Berriman Street to the Foreman house. The kids walked single file behind her, as soon as she was spied, imitating her amazing gymnastics. She knew they were having fun but maybe she didn't mind; she looked like the head of a holy funny procession proceeding to heal the sick with the aid of rubbing alcohol, musteroll, gossip and Jesus Christ. Once in Mrs. Foreman's bedroom she transformed it into a minor chaos of jars, bottles, rags, the sharp, sweet smell of alcohol, the damp, sour smell of musteroll, pieces of talk that flew in the air and dropped to the floor like confetti. Mrs. Foreman lay on her bed waiting patiently for the treatment. Mrs. Quick, after initial preparations, splashed alcohol on her hands and began by massaging Mrs. Foreman's left arm, charging up and down the cool, chestnut-colored flesh with blunt, wooden fingers. "Feel any more life in these upper muscles, Mrs. Foreman?"

"They're just about as usual."

"I don't know now, they feels suppler to me."

"I suppose it's in the hands of the Lord but the rubbing does sooth me."

"You said a mouthful, Mrs. Foreman, about the Lord. His sure are capable hands although some folks taking things into they own and making a mess of it in more ways than one," Mrs. Quick answered significantly.

"Are they?" Mrs. Foreman was listening to Coin splashing in the bathroom. "You getting along first rate, Coin," she called.

"First rate, Mama," came the reply.

"Just before I come here, Mrs. Foreman, I dropped in on Mrs. Jessup—All this is illustrating about folks taking things in their own hands, snatching the initiative away from the Lord—dropped in on her and let me tell: something got to be done. Told me that when the Dorcas Society gave their annual Fair last Saturday night, certainly am sorry I couldn't get there, that when they opened the money box at the end of the evening it were as empty as the fortune-telling teacup Flossie Green uses, yes, Mrs. Foreman, empty. Then Deaconess Redmond who had charge of it all evening commenced to scream, 'Somebody done stole the cash!' Now you know . . . the investigation's proceeding under Reverend Brooks but he's disgusted. *The Church Is Full Of Pharisees* was the text he preached upon the next morning. He called on all the God-fearing members to drive the money-changers from the temple. It were a powerful sermon. I take one exception: wasn't no exchange of money. Somebody, and I ain't mentioning who, got it all. Wasn't no exchange! Deaconess Redmond been crying ever since, saying that they scratching up her bright name. Now you know . . . course over at the Miracle Baptist Church, Reverend S. Robert Blanton take charge of the money himself, so there ain't no chance of a mistake. Talking about him, now you know you ought to get yourself on over there one of these Thursday evenings. They say he's healing the sick and most nigh raising the dead. Course that's only on Thursday nights. He keep so busy, you know." She applied musteroll to Mrs. Foreman's arm after she had finished the alcohol rub. The water was still going in the bathroom. Mrs. Quick glanced toward the door and giggled.

"He must be just about scrubbing his skin nigh off."

"He spilled ink over himself at school today."

"Now you know they getting too advanced in these New York schools. Pencil is plenty good enough," and she pinched musteroll in between Mrs. Foreman's fingers.

The house shook slightly as Woody crashed up the steps, rattling doors and tripping over furniture. Mrs. Foreman called, "Woody, wash your hands and face before you go out and help Coin get some of that ink off his."

"Okay, Mama." Mrs. Foreman could hear low talking from the bathroom and twice as much splashing.

"Getting back to Reverend S. Robert Blanton, that sure is a pretty name, one of the prettiest names I know. Don't you think so, Mrs. Foreman? 'He sure gots a pretty name,' Mrs. Jessup said before I came here. She don't always speak right English but she sure can hit the nail square on the head. Now you knows the best kind of thing you can do is to get on over there and have all these rubbings and pullings over and done with."

Coin heard silence before his mother spoke.

"Thanks, Mrs. Quick, but I haven't much faith in faithhealers."

"You'll get the faith. You got faith in our Lord, haven't you? I know you have and Reverend S. Robert Blanton works through the Lord, move your leg sideways a little bit, that's enough, and faith in the Lord pays the highest dividends especially to the sick and the afflicted. Now you knows . . . I would've hauled Mr. Quick over to see him but he dropped dead before I could get the chance. Let's see, today's Tuesday second. How about going over next Thursday in July?"

"I might go just to see what it's like."

The bathroom door opened; Coin and Woody appeared. "Now you boys want to see your Mama spry. You'd like to see your Mama walk spry, wouldn't you?"

They nodded solemnly.

"Of course you would, bless your little hearts. And that, Mrs. Foreman, is the final argument."

"Mrs. Quick, please . . ."

"Now you know I was only trying to . . ."

"Run out and play, Coin and Woody."

"You're really gonna walk straight, Mama?" Coin asked.

"You really gonna walk spry?"

"If you two don't go on out, I'll . . . I'll tell Popa when he comes home. Now scat, and Coin, tell your sister Bernice to come up here in fifteen minutes and help me get dinner."

Her voice was sharp and tender at the same time. Once he had eaten grapes from the same bunch and some were sweet and some were sour . . . now it was like that. If he could be paralyzed for his mother or maybe God would strike that Mrs. Carth.

"Mama?"

"Yes, son."

"Oh, I wasn't gonna say nothing."

Coin followed Woody downstairs. Only Woody slid down the bannisters and Coin walked down one step at a time as if he were lame. From outside the women could hear the boys calling their friend, "Abie Schneider, Abie Schneider."

Mrs. Foreman closed her eyes as Mrs. Quick worked on the thigh.

"You shouldn't have asked the children. They'll be pestering and pestering. They never noticed much before in spite of you coming twice a week . . ." her voice trailed off into a gulf. She bit her lower lip.

"I didn't mean no harm," Mrs. Quick said cheerfully.

"I know you didn't." Her good arm clutched the bedspread and held it in a tent, then let the cover wrinkle down.

"Anything wrong, Mrs. Foreman?"

"Nothing more than usual, Mrs. Quick, nothing more."

Coin wasn't paying much attention to the game of Red Rover. He tried to tag Abie Schneider and make him *it* but Abie was too fast and got away. Down the street in front of Esther's house his sister, Bernice, was jumping rope French style, with three girls. Two held the double rope and the other two bounced up and down within the whirling oval. All chanted:

I went down Fulton Ferry and I couldn't get across.
I paid a half-a-dollar for an old blind horse . . .

"Hey, Coin—it's your turn, dumbell."

"All right, Woody, I'm coming," Coin said listlessly.

"Gee whiz, if you don't want to play just say so. You're making the whole team lose."

The chanting distracted Coin and all that running and what Mrs. Quick had suggested and all. . . .

The horse wouldn't pull, I sold it for a bull.
The bull wouldn't holler, I sold it for a dollar.
The dollar wouldn't pass, I stuck it in the grass.

Is Abie a nigger? He's bad sometimes.

The grass wouldn't melt, I stuck it in my belt . . .

"You're spoiling everything. You're out, Coin."

Woody was getting so mean. There was a time when they did everything together but now he was always racing around and saying dirty rhymes and kicking Abie in the shin when he wouldn't mind him. Woody had always been the head of the kids on the block and they all did whatever he said because he had all the ideas. He loved Woody better than anybody. Well, he didn't care. He wanted to sit on the curb anyhow. There were things to get straightened out. His thoughts were that roller coaster in Luna Park zipping up and down and around. Mama hadn't liked what Mrs. Quick said but just the same suppose . . . maybe God could do something. Popa always said that He worked in those mysterious ways, His wonders to perform. Tonight he'd pray. Maybe Woody would pray too. Mrs. Quick knew a thing or two . . . all sorts of things happened that you didn't expect. Mrs. Quick should know, she was always hanging around God . . .

The belt was too narrow, I stuck it on a sparrow,
The sparrow wouldn't fly, I stuck it in the sky . . .

Coin turned his head toward the jumping jacks and remembered that he had to tell Bernice. He cupped his hands and called, "Bernice."

"What?"

"Mama wants you."

"All right," she called back in disgust. "Oh, you made me miss. Wait till I get you upstairs. You're a pain in the neck."

First Woody and now Bernice. He could only talk to Mama. Bernice was yelling like a wild Indian, you could hear her up and down the street. "I've gotta go upstairs so I've gotta take my rope."

Esther pleaded, "Let us keep it for a while. I'll supervise it personally." She pronounced each word very distinctly because she was going to be a schoolteacher when she grew up. Coin was in her class after regular school. He liked Esther.

"It's my rope and I can't leave it with nobody."

"You're mean Bernice as . . . as . . . well as Miss Binatree."

"I don't care," replied Bernice snatching the rope from Esther and carefully winding it around her arm like a snake bracelet from armpit to wrist and back again.

Bernice is a nigger, Coin decided for the second time that afternoon. After his sister had gone into the house, Esther came over and sat down on the curb beside Coin.

"Do you want to play school, Coin? I got a new blackboard for my birthday."

"When was that?"

"Yesterday. Do you want to?"

"No."

"I have all colors of chalk," Esther tempted daintily. Coin didn't want to think about school after what had happened earlier.

"I don't like school any more."

"Oh," she said looking into his dark big eyes, "oh."

Coin answered with a blink and then a long stare. He wished he could tell her about everything—instead he started to count the freckles on her nose. One side at a time and then the middle. It took a long time. His mouth, his fingers recorded his halting count.

"Coin."

"Shhhhhhhhhh," he hissed. He kept counting till she turned her face away. Then there was a long pause while he made a total. "One hundred and twenty-three," he said finally and took a long breath.

"A hundred and twenty-three what?"

"A hundred and twenty-three freckles on your nose."

She began to cry. Coin leaned toward her. "I didn't mean nothing, Esther." She moved her head farther away and started to rise.

"Where are you going?"

"Home to wash them off."

He held her hand. "Don't cry, Esther."

She wiped her tears on the back of her wrist and then began the prettiest smile in the world. A little freckled sun. "Esther?" he mocked tentatively.

"What snot ten cents a whole lot." They both laughed convulsively. Esther stopped first.

"That's a very bad word, Coin. It is not very nice."

"Woody says it all the time." They began to laugh again and kept it up until Coin noticed Mrs. Quick hopping out his house.

"Mrs. Quick?"

"Now you know I didn't see you there, child. I declare my eyes are playing all sorts of tricks." Coin walked over to her slowly; tiptoed to whisper in her ear.

"Is Mama going to the meeting?"

"I don't know rightly but I think with a little encouragement . . . and the Lord is on our side."

"I'm going to let Agnes know, huh?"

"You do that, son."

Coin followed behind her as she moved away rapidly. Hop, skip and jump and a little old black bag; hop, skip and jump and a little old black bag. Then he ran behind Esther, who was watching the Red Rover game, put his hands over her eyes and whispered, "Guess who?"

"You that's who I knew boo hoo."

Coin was satisfied with the answer. "I'll play school Monday, Esther, if Miss Raidin doesn't keep me in."

"What were you talking to the nurse about?"

"It's a secret," cried Coin bouncing into the vestibule of his house.

Before supper was almost the best time of all. Nobody said a thing about homework. Dinner cooking smelled good. Ordinarily he would be playing funeral or old witch with Popa's black and orange bathrobe. But Woody was still in the street and he didn't feel like playing all by himself, so he lay on the low-down bed and stared at the ceiling. He'd make pictures from the cracks and faint brown and gray blurs. Popa said that if you looked at the stars hard enough you'd find all kinds of pictures. You might even see a big dipper scooping up the dark in the sky. Once he'd looked real hard and didn't see any of these things, so he gave up the stars. Yes, he preferred the ceiling. No pictures came out for him immediately today. Must be cloudy in the ceiling. He turned two somersaults, then stopped when he heard the front door slam. Agnes was home. Substitute teaching all day out in Bay Ridge made her irritable just before dinnertime so he had learned to keep quiet until she thawed out. If he got over that period without a slap, she would probably read to the whole family after they ate. That was the best time of all.

"Mama," he heard Agnes say, "do you know what? That girl is outside wheeling her baby carriage in front of our house as if she were picketing us."

"Did you speak to her, Agnes?"

"Of course not; that would give her too much satisfaction . . ."

"I declare, your brother Oscar will be the death of me yet. I'll have to ask Popa to speak to him, he's disgracing the whole family."

"That girl is!" replied Agnes unhesitatingly.

"She's out there every day when I come home from school," Bernice put in. "I don't like her one bit."

"No one asked you for your two cents' worth, Bernice."

"Oh, shut up, Agnes, I was just telling you."

"Mama," Agnes complained, "do I have to come home after a hard day's work and listen to all this?"

"Bernice," Mrs. Foreman said quietly, "I think the stew is almost done. Look at it. Bernice, please don't leave your skates and jumping rope in the middle of the floor where anyone can trip over them."

Mrs. Foreman and Agnes were talking more quietly now. "She was in Bernice's class last term. I don't know how a girl that age could possibly . . ."

"She's fourteen," Mrs. Foreman sighed.

"And Oscar's sixteen. I thought Popa got it all straightened out when he went to court."

"He did, Agnes. She's just trying to humiliate us. Leave her alone. God knows Popa hasn't one cent to give her." There was a pause before Mrs. Foreman spoke again. "I wish we could send him away to one of those schools. He's getting worse every day. I don't think he'll graduate at the end of the month. And he stays out so late and won't mind . . ."

"Anything wrong, Mama?"

"No. I just felt dizzy."

"Why don't you lie down?" Agnes' voice was so quiet now. They hadn't even mentioned the ink.

"Besides, Popa will be home soon. I want to be on my feet when he comes in. Agnes, Coin spilled ink all over his suit at school today. He had to empty ink from one of those big bottles into a small well."

Now it was coming. He began to scrunch in his toes. Well, he just wouldn't cry when Agnes slapped him.

"Teachers shouldn't send a boy that age after ink. Those bottles are so awkward . . ."

He wasn't going to get a slap after all. She was thinking about the problem of Oscar and ink was nothing when it came to thinking about Oscar. In a way he was sorry because he was prepared to take the punishment and now he'd have to wait until Popa came home and he was sure to notice even if they didn't say one word. Agnes' slap was nothing to Popa's strap. Funny thing that Oscar never got a whipping. Maybe because he was named after Popa: Oscar Emerson Foreman, Junior.

Popa liked to call him by the whole name. Each time it sounded like a roll call in school: a lot of first names run together. Maybe Oscar was too strong for Popa. No, Popa wasn't afraid of anything or anybody. Not even Mr. Courtland, and he worked for him. Coin had heard his father laying Mr. Courtland to rest plenty of times after supper for sending him to Long Island for strawberries or something from a hothouse right in the middle of winter. Or that night he had to go to Washington unexpectedly and was forced to postpone his installation as president of the Society of the Sons of Virginia. Did Popa curse then! He must've been mad. Hell and damn, he had snapped out, because of Mr. Courtland. Popa didn't fear Oscar. Coin glanced up suddenly at the ceiling and was sure he saw Oscar's face just as plain, or was it a bulldog? Closing his eyes he counted to seventeen, opened them again. Yes, that was his brother all right and he was laughing down at him brown and gray. Coin gaped back real hard but Oscar wouldn't stop laughing. So he crossed his eyes to the ceiling with glee and stuck his tongue out for good measure.

"Dear Heavenly Father, make us truly grateful for this food which we are about to receive for the nourishment of our bodies, for this and all other blessings, we ask it in the name of Thy Son, Christ Jesus, who died on the cross that we might live. Amen." Mr. Foreman invariably said grace in megaphone tones. To Coin he sounded like he was praying before the whole Sunday school or wanted Mrs. Renaldo upstairs to hear or the Bernsteins across the airshaft to bow their heads with Agnes and Mama and Woody and Bernice and sometimes Oscar. The loud, deep tobacco voice signified prayer over more than a simple stew. The comport seemed to grow large enough to include fried chicken, corn on the cob, candied sweets, rice, ice cream, walnut cake and all. The crisp eager amen caused every sort of good juice to flow in his mouth. His father prayed over mountains of food and every kind was Coin's favorite. The gaslight spreading shadows and highlights around the room helped reinforce other illusions too. For instance, Popa's diploma from Wayland Seminary was a window, in the misty corner near the kitchen door, reflecting wrinkled gaslights: like three little moons wavering over Popa's name there; the walls, with the ugly red and purple flowers in a green field, faded into mysterious owl forests; the picture of the last judgment above the buffet appreciated the prayer and Christ's outstretched hands suffered little children to come unto Him, instead of striking at the wicked in their downward fall.

"Momps," his voice had a little bit of ha-ha in it, "where's the napkins?" He reared back in his chair, smiling.

Of course they didn't have any, but Popa seemed to think so and that Mama was just too stingy to use them.

"They're in the same place, Popa."

"Bernice, fetch the napkins."

Bernice went to the buffet and took nothing out of the top drawer and handed each one some air shaped like a napkin. Coin thought that was the biggest joke!

As Mr. Foreman lifted the covering to the comport and sniffed lima bean stew, Woody leaned over to Coin and whispered:

> *Beans, beans, the musical fruit,*
> *The more you eat, the more you poot.*

Nobody heard for Mr. Foreman's mouth worked out large fat ohs and ahs.

"Momps," he called, "this smells mighty tempting. Might be forced to take a second helping. Yes-sir-re-Bob, I might be forced to do that." Steam smoked his small black hedge of mustache. The two boys still giggled over their rhyme and Bernice joined them after repeating yes-sir-re-Bob in what she thought was a deep voice; her upper teeth thrust forward, catching the light, gave her an extra lip, white and slick. The three of them just couldn't stop laughing. The ritual Mr. Foreman made out of serving the food always delighted them. He called out each name as a plate was passed to its destination. When he said, "Coin, pass this to your mother," Woody and Coin screamed with new, unfounded mirth until their mother said that she couldn't eat that much. "Just a spoonful, that's all I want." Mr. Foreman unloaded the plate commenting that she should eat more. "Strength doesn't grow in the air. Course I know you're one of those tasters while you cook but just the same . . ."

Only Coin knew the secret of Mama's small appetite.

He and his mother were unspoken allies. Woody had been in the house when Mrs. Renaldo brought food but he was too busy making fun to really catch on to what it meant. Coin had caught on three weeks ago. He never spoke about it, but the secret was Mama's and his, like a letter written in a special ink only they could see. Mrs. Renaldo had knocked at the door and he had run to answer.

"Is your mother home?" she whispered in Italian.

Coin couldn't understand her language and he often amused himself with translations of what he thought the foreign words signified. Of course "is your mother home" was simple because her voice ended upward and she wouldn't be asking for anyone else anyway. Her voice was low, saying prayers all the time. He was a little bit afraid of this woman who lived alone upstairs, who always dressed in black. (Old skirt went past her ankles and just licked up the dust when she walked along.) He wondered if she wore that long veil, attached to her hair with dark combs, to bed. On the street it flew behind her like black wind. Her eyes were tiny and dim, but when she spoke they lit up and came toward you bright and dangerous like auto lights running up the street in the dark. No body, just lights. Her face had no in between color, black and white. And she went to the cemetery every Sunday as regularly as he went to church. He asked his mother about that and she had answered, "All her family lives there, she visits them just like your Aunt Harriet or Lucy Horwitz visits us."

"But we talk to them, Mama, and they talk back and

eat with us and bring presents besides. Nobody's out there where she goes, I bet, except old stones and grass."

His mother's eyes closed for a second and her face didn't move, not one muscle. She might be going to sleep. "But they're with her," and her face became alive again.

"Is your mother home?" Mrs. Renaldo said.

"Yes," Coin replied, "in the dining room."

"Come in, Mrs. Renaldo."

The magenia smell came with her. Magenia was his and Woody's name for the Italian smell: garlic, spaghetti, red pepper, damp flour, all smothered in the dish she held in front of her. Smothered but alive in Coin's nose. She entered the dining room like a black ghost. Not a regular ghost in dreams but ghost of some kind, thin bird that never in its life was able to sing a song. Coin thought that but didn't understand what he thought one bit.

Mrs. Renaldo set the dish on the oak table and sat down in the rocker facing his mother. They spoke together: his mother in English, Mrs. Renaldo in Italian. They understood each other through the eyes. That's what he knew. Going out the birdghost hugged him with musty magenia wings and he withdrew gently. Soft claws patted his head. The prayer voice repeated something and the door closed without noise.

Now Coin sensed that his mother ate food that all hated, so that they would have enough. He knew she hated that old food too but forced it down like castor oil. He knew all that, yet he danced about his mother with Woody and laughed at her eating magenia food. What Woody did, he did, and it made no sense at all.

"Look at Mama eating that old stinking stuff," Woody had laughed, nudged Coin and continued, "I wouldn't eat that for nobody. Would you?"

"Sure smells bad," Coin agreed.

"Whoo wheeeeeeeee. Smells like rotting-away potatoes. Huh, Coin?"

"Sure does."

"Smells like a nanny goat," danced Woody.

"Mama, don't eat that stuff."

"You'll get poisoned."

"You boys go on and play." His mother's voice was very quiet.

"Com'on Coin, let's call Abie."

"Yes, he's got a new scooter."

"I'm gonna ride first," Coin had yelled.

"Nope, I'm gonna."

"You boys toss a coin." Was she saying something else?

"I ain't got a penny but we'll choose fingers."

Fingers shot out: odds, evens, odds, odds. "I win," Woody was opening the door, "ohoooooooooo wheeeeeeee that sure smells bad."

"Smells like somebody broke wind," Coin tried to outdo his brother.

"Smells like nunie," Woody called back.

"Mama, don't eat that stuff," were the last words Coin said before he started toward the opened door.

He hesitated, then quickly ran back to his mother, kissed her right on the cheek.

In the whiz of sliding down the bannister he heard his mother call, "Coin, you broke Mrs. Renaldo's bowl."

"Areyacoming, Coin?" Woody cried impatiently from outside.

"I'm coming," Coin cried back.

Now through all his giggling he recalled that and looked at his mother calmly sitting there and wondered why he wasn't crying. He'd think about it tonight before he went to sleep.

"Momps, looks like the boys got little laughing machines in their throats." Pleased with his joke, he beamed around the table. "Pass this to your sister Agnes, Bernice." He always said your mother or your sister or your brother, as if they didn't know who was who. They howled.

Mr. Foreman finished his first spoonful of stew, smacked his lips and withdrew from his vest pocket the largest handkerchief Coin ever saw, tucked it into his high, stiff collar and declared, "Yes, I think I'll have to dish me up a second helping before long."

Mrs. Foreman smiled pale blue and asked Agnes to refill the comport when Popa finished serving.

"How did your day go, Momps?"

"Nothing unusual. Mrs. Quick came . . ." Coin glanced up from his plate. "Mama's gonna walk straight. Mrs. Quick said so. We've all gotta pray."

"Coin, I wish you'd speak when you're spoken

to . . ." Agnes set the refilled comport in front of her father.

"Is that so, Momps? Coin, your mother hasn't lacked for prayers. The Lord works in His own way . . ."

"His wonders to perform," Agnes continued.

Woody paused, turned his full spoon upside down and let beans and tomatoes plop into his plate before he said, "The Lord's not going to do it . . . Reverend Blanton's gonna . . . Thursday. That's what Mrs. Quick said."

"I promised to tell Agnes," Coin whispered as if his throat were filled with mush.

Mr. Foreman twinkled, "Better to tell me, Coin, your sister Agnes doesn't find time for church these days."

Everybody looked at Bernice when she began a fresh display of giggling. With so much attention tied to her as if she were a Maypole, Coin knew they couldn't help pulling the ribbons.

"I know why Agnes doesn't go to church on Sundays. . . ." Her words danced out for expectant partners.

"We're all in the family," Mr. Foreman urged with a large wink toward his wife, "we can keep a secret."

"Well, last Sunday I saw . . ." Bernice jerked forward suddenly, "well, never mind but," she shot a look at Agnes, "I know." Agnes kept on eating.

"Don't tease so, Bernice. We all know about Harry," Mrs. Foreman said quietly.

"Momps, what about Mrs. Quick and Reverend Blanton?"

Woody answered for her. "I just told you, he's holding miracle meetings. Mama's going with Mrs. Quick."

"That's right," Coin still didn't look up from his plate. Mr. Foreman cleared his throat and Coin knew something special was coming.

"Coin, you and Woody seem mighty concerned with prayer and preachers. I suppose you'll both be trotting up when they open the doors of the church this Sunday for those who want to dedicate their lives to the Lord." It really was a question but Coin couldn't think of any answer. His father turned to Woody. "How about you, son?"

Woody tickled his brother's thigh under the table and then pinched it real hard as he gravely answered, "I haven't seen the little man yet."

"You will if you think long enough and pray hard." Mr. Foreman was so positive about it that Coin suspected that the little man was lurking in the wallpaper forest or would squirm out of the last judgment picture. Maybe he'll see the little man before Sunday and could sit on the mourners' bench. But where? What shape? What color? What language?

If he became a real Christian, God might listen to his prayers for Mama. His face must have a funny look because Agnes was watching him so hard, maybe reading his thoughts, so he asked for a second helping and determined not to think about it until she wasn't there. His father was watching Agnes watching him.

He helped Coin's plate and his eyes twinkled when he said, "Agnes, I think you're too hard on the Lord. He has always provided and He always will. Isn't that right, Momps?"

Mrs. Foreman replied that he was right, and that brought a satisfied look into his eyes. Coin wondered why his mother had hesitated so before she answered but when Agnes put her knife and fork neatly on her plate, drew her lips in, sucked them with her tongue, Coin stopped wondering. Agnes had something to say that just couldn't wait.

"I wish He'd do something about that girl of Oscar's who parades up and down in front of the house every afternoon with her carriage. I don't know what kind of trouble she's going to start. And we never know where Oscar is or what he's up to. That's more important than Coin and Woody's seeing that little man." Her words had pebbles in them and each one hit Popa in a different part of his face.

"Agnes, that's a hard way to talk to your father." Mrs. Foreman put her good hand to her trembling mouth, then lowered it to stroke her paralyzed left fingers.

"That's all right, Momps, I'm used to hearing Agnes being disrespectful."

"I'm not disrespectful. I just wish you'd face the truth once in a while instead of putting everything on the Lord, Popa."

Mr. Foreman worked his lips in and out before he said, "Daught, you may leave the table."

Everything got so still. Coin thought he heard a little hiss and puff from the lights. Mr. Foreman folded his handkerchief carefully. Coin was mad at Agnes. Just when Popa was in a good mood she had to go and spoil it. Bernice squirmed into a low nervous giggle.

"I'm sorry, Popa," Agnes finally said and stayed in her chair.

"Thank you, daught. I want all my children to become Christians. That's what I meant to say."

Coin wanted to cry out to them to stop it, stop it, look at Mama, look at Mama, she's not feeling good, look at Mama. But he kept his mouth shut.

"It hasn't helped Oscar much and he was the first one to go up." Agnes smiled as if she had swallowed a joke and Coin thought that she was the biggest nigger of them all. If Oscar was a Christian why did he act so bad sometimes and then like last Sunday night he had preached a sermon for all of them in the parlor and Popa had laughed saying that Oscar was going to be a regular preacher someday. At least one of the family was dedicated. How was that? But Oscar was real funny standing behind a turned-around chair for a pulpit, imitating Reverend Brooks jumping like a jack-in-the-box up and down, shouting about hell flames and burning down the wicked. He had put his hands on his shoulder blades and waved them to make-believe angels flying past the morning stars to eternal suppers of manna. Popa said regular, too-loud amens, patting his foot. And Agnes needn't be so smart, she was there too, playing the piano and singing the hymns with the rest of them, she was acting like in a play and took little bows after each song. Mama didn't join in but Mrs. Quick, looking like an unmade bed, screamed hallelujah just like she was in regular church and even got up to "testify to His goodness tonight because He's helped me." She was serious and her big bosom swelled up like blowing out cheeks from her chest. Her behind bounced on the davenport. They were making fun and they weren't making fun. He wished he could ask his mother all about that and the little man when nobody else was around.

Mr. Foreman rested both elbows on the table and leaned forward, staring at Agnes real hard. Agnes stared back. Something made Coin scared and he wanted to be outside punching Abie or somebody or watching Esther cry. He began scraping a scab just below his right knee. He knew he shouldn't do that because it would bleed and hurt. Bleed and hurt and Mama look what I done to my knee. Just look.

At first Coin couldn't figure out how the blood had gotten from his knee to the pillowcase when he woke up in the middle of the night. Then he remembered the pillow fight with Woody just before bed. Woody sure could throw a mean pillow. Coin wasn't scared of the dark. Not this dark anyhow. He knew this dark. He heard his father's sucking snores and his mother's breathing from across the room. Why did grown people always make noises in their sleep? Woody didn't make a sound but he pulled covers and kicked. The clock on the dresser was good company: all those bright-green numbers standing in the air. Was it two o'clock or ten past twelve? He leaned closer to look and almost rolled out of bed. He was sleepy again so he lay just as he was with his head touching the floor. The blood rushing around his eyes and behind his ears woke him up again. He forced his head to the pillow. That was better. The dot of fire was still there below his kneecap. He felt a new scab growing. Oscar's face disappeared from the ceiling. Had he said his regular prayers before? Mama had gone to bed so early and Popa talked to Agnes so late. Well, he'd say them again to make sure. Of course he didn't have to get out of bed and he could whisper low like Mrs. Renaldo.

"Now I lay me down to sleep, I pray the Lord my soul to keep; God bless Mama and Popa, sisters and brother, all my friends; help me to be a good boy, amen." The special prayer for his mother would have to wait until he saw the little man and sat on the mourners' bench tomorrow. Anyway he really didn't know what to say except make his mother's arm and leg like everybody else's. It was funny tonight, during the pillow fight he had heard Agnes say that Mama became sick right after he was born. But how was that? She didn't have anything to do with it according to Popa's story. Like all the other seven children he had been ordered through Dr. Henry. Only he was the last one and had come on a cold December morning at exactly eight o'clock in a black bag, kicking up a fuss. That's what Popa said. Coin asked if he had come special delivery and Popa just laughed and laughed. He laughed too. But it went back to the same thing. How had he made his mother sick? If that was true then everything was his fault and Sunday was as important as could be. He'd ask her about it all. She would tell him the truth. Everything was sleeping now. Popa's noise was less and less. Woody hadn't kicked for the longest time. The clock numbers weren't half so sharp. The green song of hands and bright, still ticked in his ears pleasantly. Sleep and wish. Wish and sleep. He rested one hand on the warm dot below his knee and deliberately pulled all the covers off Woody with the other. Then he closed his eyes and tried to make a dream.

When the pounding began, Coin's body jerked into a knot. He lay stiff and scared. He couldn't tell if the trembling all around was part of his sleep or if he was awake. The bed started to shimmy. He wanted to holler out or shake Woody. But he couldn't move his hands or his feet and his tongue was folded between his teeth. He was awake all right. It was Oscar beating outside on the wall next to his parent's bed. Opening one eye he saw Mr. Foreman get out of bed, put on the thick bathrobe and grope through the dining room to the front door. He heard his mother crying in the dark and the voices of Oscar and father far away speaking in low anger.

"How many times have I told you not to pound the whole house awake in the middle of the night. I'll tear your little behind to pieces next time you . . ."

"You better not touch me," Oscar's voice was thick and hoarse and had daggers in it.

"Listen, boy, your mother and I have endured enough

of this. What kind of example is this for your brothers."

"Why don't you give me a key?"

"No sixteen-year-old boy needs a key. You'll be home and ready for bed by ten o'clock hereafter or I'll know the reason why. And I want you to stay away from that girl. God knows I moved heaven and earth to get you out of that trouble. What in the world's gotten into you, boy?" There was a long pause and a faint cracking sound in the walls and a tickling sound like mice. "Answer me, boy?"

"Aw," Oscar grunted.

"Your mother tells me you probably won't graduate. You can't get anywhere without education. What do you want to be, a janitor, or wait on other people all your life?"

"Aw."

"Have you got the lockjaw?"

"Humh, aw."

"Now get to bed. I'll attend to you in the morning."

"You'd better not touch me. Take your hand offa my arm, you."

"Stop that shouting. Who do you think you're talking to—some of those good-for-nothing friends of yours? Your mother's sick. God knows what the boys would think if they heard you."

Coin could tell them. Oscar was a nigger and he looked like a bulldog with purple dimples and bulging eyes and no taller than a highchair. And . . . and . . . He heard his mother crying in the dark . . . and his feet stank like down in the sewer. Yes they did. His stockings were stiff and they stank too, and the next time he saw him he was going to spit. And he was skinny because he smoked Sweet Caporal cigarettes. And he did number one in the alley beside Esther's house. Woody saw him do it. Well, he was no snitcher but if Popa asked him what he thought he'd just tell, that was all, and Woody knew too, so there.

"Stop that shouting, Oscar Emerson Foreman, Junior. Now mark me, boy. . . . Are you listening?"

"I'm marking." He sounded like he was making fun of Popa.

Coin heard his father's hand hit Oscar's face. Wham. There was another wham and a third and a fourth. Wham, wham. "You'll be respectful if I have to knock the liver out of you. I'm sorry I had to strike you, son. I've never lost my temper like that with any of my children but you've got to learn, you've got to stop worrying your mother. Now go to bed and get hold of yourself. You've been acting like a crazy lunatic long enough and it's got to stop."

He heard his mother crying in the dark. The solid shadow of his father, crouching into bed breathing hard, was over there. Oscar, bent way down low, with his head in his hands grunting like Mrs. Carth's dog when Davey used his stick, moved through the bedroom to his cot in the back parlor. In a little while Coin heard him snoring long and short with a whistle in between.

IF YOU touch the hump on her back, it'll bring you good luck, you know that," said Woody applying jet oil to his Sunday shoes. "You're not afraid of that old Deaconess Westerfield, are you?"

Coin wasn't afraid but he had his doubts about the good luck part.

"Touching her hump's not going to help me see the little man. You're just being so smart because you won't tell me what he looks like. I don't think you saw him at all. You're making it up." Coin was trying to knot his stockings so that they wouldn't wrinkle down in church. The time was coming near and Woody wouldn't give him a hint and he hadn't dreamt no little man last night. How could he? All that was going on.

> *Holy, holy, holy,*
> *Lord God Almighty,*
> *Early in the morning*
> *The sun shall rise to Thee . . .*

The song burst out of the bathroom door so loud and happy that Coin began to doubt that anything had happened at all last night. And Oscar had been at the breakfast table and said his verse for the day just like the rest of them. Of course his selection was the shortest in the Bible: Jesus Wept, John 11:35. And there hadn't been any scars on his face either. Popa sure sang big:

> *Cherabim and Seraphim*
> *Falling down before him . . .*

Cherabim and Seraphim certainly must be funny with names like that. Maybe all that pounding and talking was only a dream. Seraphim. He felt better.

"You're just afraid," said Woody. "I touch it a lot of times when she's sitting in the amen-pew. Me and PeeWee Taylor sometimes. I brush up against her or say Deaconess Westerfield, you got a piece of lint on your back. And she says, where, take it off, son, and I just touch that old hump and she says, thank you, son. Last Sunday she give me a gum drop." Woody was smiling red. Why didn't he call me instead of that shrimp PeeWee? "It's easy. Do something like that."

"She'll know."

"Gee whiz, can't you think up a thing by yourself?"

Bernice called from the dining room. "You'd better hurry. Popa's almost ready."

> God in three persons,
> Blessed Trinity.

The song was still in the air and Coin wondered if blessed trinity had anything to do with the church downtown called Holy Trinity. Suddenly he felt cool air on his left heel. "Look, Woody, I got a big hole in my stocking."

Woody looked up. "That's nothing. I'll fix it so nobody'll notice in a million years." He dipped the long-tongued stopper into the bottle and swabbed Coin's skin at the heel with the wet, black polish. Woody always could think up something. But when Coin looked down he noticed that the part of his skin that had been dyed was drying shiny and didn't match the stocking dullness at all.

Woody thought up something else. "Pull your stocking down and lump the holey part into your shoes." It made a big pucker but it wasn't too bad at all.

They went into the living room where Mrs. Foreman was sitting by the window waiting to inspect them. Her eyes went up and down before she said that they looked fine and that the ink-stained pants of Coin's Mr. Altar had dyed came out almost like new.

"I like them now, Mama." She hadn't noticed.

"Okay, Mama?" said Woody.

"Okay." Mrs. Foreman answered putting her good arm about them. "All right now, your father's waiting."

Woody raced out but Coin couldn't move an inch. She'd notice for sure if he turned around, so he began to back out. He felt the lump in his heel unlump and the cool air return.

"Coin, what in the world's the matter with you?"

"Nothing, Mama. I like to walk backwards sometimes. And Miss Radin says it's good for balance."

"I believe you're trying to hide something. Turn round."

"No, I'm not."

"Then turn round."

Coin turned around.

"Take that stocking off. The idea of going to church with a hole in your heel as big as a lemon. And trying to fool me. Why, Coin!"

"I haven't got any others."

"Well, you can't wear those." She thought for a moment and smiled. "Did you put that polish on your heel?"

"Well, I . . . well, yes I did."

Then they laughed together a little bit; it was so funny trying to fool Mama's eagle eye.

"I believe Oscar's got a clean extra pair you can put on," his mother said releasing him.

All last night was true. In a flash he heard his mother crying in the dark and smelled Oscar's stinking feet.

"No, I don't want his dirty old stockings."

"They're clean."

"Please Mama."

"Your father's waiting. Do as you're told."

"They're too big."

"Big or small, it's better than that hole."

"Do I have to, Mama?"

"Yes."

"Can't Agnes sew mine?"

"There isn't time."

"Then," pouted Coin, "I'll stay home."

"Momps, is Coin ready?" Popa threw his voice into the living room like a big round ball scaring him, but Mama caught it.

"In a minute." She turned to Coin. "There's nothing wrong with the stockings and Oscar won't mind."

"Don't make me wear them, Mama. Don't make me do that . . . I . . . I just don't want to. . . ." He thought he was going to cry but when he looked into his mother's face, tired and pale, he knew she didn't know that he was awake in the dark while she wept like Jesus and his father comforted her.

"Momps, Momps, don't take on so, Momps. I didn't mean to hit the boy so hard."

"It's not that, not only that. So much came up today. Agnes . . . her nerves are like rags, she has to give so much into the house and gets so little in return. And she wants to marry Harry. . . ."

"Momps, Momps, Mr. Courtland gave me dinner money . . . five dollars extra . . . that will help some . . . a little. Somewhere, somehow, the Lord will provide."

"Mrs. Carth called Coin a nigger. Imagine calling a little boy that. I didn't know what to say. It's going to break my heart, Popa, I didn't know what to say . . ."

He felt his mother weeping in the dark.

". . . and the boys heard Mrs. Quick. . . . How am I going to answer the boys?"

Coin answered her to himself so soft it was brushing feathers together: pray Mama, pray like Mrs. Quick said and go to be healed.

"That's all right, Momps. We'll be all right . . . get some rest . . . tomorrow's Sunday. Another Sunday. Goodnight, goodnight, Momps. . . ."

"Goodnight, Popa."

All the goodnights swamped Coin as he looked at his mother now and reached up, not knowing why, touched around her eyes as if he wanted to wipe away tears already dried. His family was in trouble.

He leaned against her remembering too how she had dragged her left foot more than usual this morning frying the johnnycake to make them happy, mending the night before with big slabs of fried dough for her children on Sunday morning. And Oscar didn't matter now anyway or his old socks. Coin was ashamed to cause so much fuss over something that was last night away and this was the morning, the going up morning and that night he could pray and be heard if all went okay. And Seraphim.

Mrs. Foreman called at last, "The boys are both ready. Go ahead, Coin."

"I'll put the stockings on, I didn't mean nothing."

"Go on ahead. It won't make much difference. One hole." Coin smiled as Woody flew in and, without stopping, grabbed his hand and they ran out of the living room, through the bedroom and past their father in the kitchen, smelling of Sunday, in his blue serge suit.

"Com'on, Bernice," Woody grabbed her hand happily, "you slow poke." And the three of them dashed down the steps into the quiet Sunday street.

From the window on the second floor Mrs. Foreman waved goodbye to her retreating children; only Coin gazed back, but in the split-second look at his mother's face, trembling in pale golden light, he saw something; he saw *him*, the little man, there behind her, hovering over her hair, supporting her arm too. The mystery of this recognition sent a tremble through his body.

"Com'on, slow poke."

Coin caught up with Woody and Bernice. He glanced back once again but his mother's face was in darkness and there was nothing around her at all. Now he wanted to hold the memory in mind so hard he could draw it. He didn't even notice Esther on her porch or hear her say, "Hello, Coin."

Or Bernice mocking, "Your girl friend's calling you, Coin." If he had it wouldn't have made any difference, he'd seen a mystery just as plain. That was more than Woody had seen because, if he had, how could he talk about it over jet oil.

Woody, Bernice and Coin went to the Montaulk station directly. Mr. Foreman went by way of Atkins Avenue. When the children reached Pitkin Avenue they waited for him in front of Grant's Ice Cream Parlor gazing at the piled-up plates of Tootsie Rolls, lemon drops, brown and black licorice twists, peanut brittle, chocolate drops and all-day suckers in green, red, yellow, orange and black.

"I'll buy some with my Sunday collection money," conspired Woody, "and give you some, if you won't tell."

The memory of the little man had taken a firm grip on Coin and if he was going to be a real Christian he might as well start now. He said, "No, and I will tell."

"You're the biggest sissy of them all," Woody snarled and Bernice echoed.

They spied Mr. Foreman a block away walking the step that made his head nod back and forward as if he were saying a never-ending series of howdoyoudo, howdoyoudos. He was smoking a big long cigar. They all began to giggle. That's why Popa always sent them ahead. At half a block away they watched him stub out his cigar, stop to cut off the fire end with his pearl penknife, wipe his mouth with his handkerchief, plop a piece of gum into his mouth and pace his gait more rapidly.

They raced across the street and, pausing under the shed at the foot of the steps, Woody read the advertisement enameled in blue and white on each riser: EX LAX.

"The last one up's a bum," he yelled, permitting himself a headstart. Bernice and Coin repeated alternately as they dashed up:

47

"Ex."
"Lax."
"Ex."
"Lax."

Woody arrived at the head of the steps first. Bernice was second. Coin was a bum. Bernice leaned against the railing overlooking rooftops and read from the huge sign on the Montaulk Theatre: CHILDREN CRY FOR CHAS. H. FLETCHER'S CASTORIA.

"I bet it tastes like poison," Woody commented.

"I wonder what's taking Popa so long."

"What's Castoria?" asked Coin.

"Well, it's something I never cried for," Bernice said, "and if I did, I never got it."

"It tastes like poison," Woody repeated.

It means castor oil, Coin decided.

Bernice was reading something else. COMING, COMING RUDOLPH VALENTINO IN THE SHEIK WITH AGNES AYRES. She sighed dreamily.

The cashier in the cage beside the turnstile smiled as Bernice, standing tiptoe to look grown-up, plunked three nickels down and waited for Coin and Woody to snap through. Bernice smiled back at the lady whose eyes followed the two boys out of the door onto the platform.

"They'd be cute," she said, "if they were white."

"They're cute already." Bernice's smile faded and her upper lip touched her nose. Then she joined the boys.

"What did she say?" Woody asked.

"How do I know, the old prune face," Bernice said. But she didn't talk much on the way to church.

Mr. Foreman read his Bible. Woody went to the front of the car to watch the tracks and figure out why they always looked like they were coming together in the distance, but when the train got there they were apart and the tracks ahead were coming together. Coin had seen the little man, and he was ready to tell the deacons what he had seen, when the time came, in the room behind the baptismal pool.

Mr. Foreman was exasperated because the Redmond family, "you'd think they had founded the Corinthian Baptist, they were so bold," were comfortable in the third row to the left of the pulpit where the Foremans usually sat.

"You'd think they'd know better, the crazy lunatics, as long as we've been sitting in those pews. Some people haven't got the sense they were born with."

Bernice said, "Maybe they didn't think we were coming." Mr. Foreman told her to keep quiet. "Use your energy to go down there and tell Deaconess Redmond that those seats were taken and have been for the last twenty-five years, each and every Sunday."

"Oh, Popa!"

"Do as I say, child."

"But Popa."

"Just tell them politely that Deacon O. E. Foreman said so and that you're his daughter."

"They know who I am already. She might do it if you ask her."

"I've got to get my gloves and badge. You boys go with your sister." And he went down the far aisle toward the deacons' room.

"Not me," Woody said.

"I'll stay with Woody," Coin said.

"You're both fraidy cats and dumboxes." And she switched down to the amen pew. Even from where Coin stood watching Bernice argue with Deaconess Redmond, he knew she was winning. Her mouth went like clapping hands. Bernice didn't let her get a word in edgeways or any other way. Pretty soon Deaconess Redmond was gathering her coat, Bible and pocketbook together. She was some mad, she didn't even bother to straighten her hat with the big white roses that was tilted to one side. She almost flung her children into the aisle and they departed.

"From whence they came like a holy ghost," Bernice giggled when she described the incident. "I did what Popa said with a few extra reasons and it worked like magic."

"I told you it would." Mr. Foreman seemed so pleased, he didn't even comment on the use of holy ghost.

"Spread out a little bit," Woody whispered to Coin. "Here comes Sister Hopskipandjump and I bet she's gonna try to squeeze in." But before they knew it Mrs. Quick was squeezing in.

"Good Morning, Deacon Foreman. It certainly is nice

to see you and the children. How is Mrs. Foreman? Oh, she's a brave soldier, that's what I was telling Mrs. Jessup before I came here. She's ailing, too. You boys don't mind if I just ease in here. Thank you. Coin, you sure are getting big. Isn't he growing up fine for his age? And he's the spit and image of you. Mrs. Jessup says he favors Mrs. Foreman but I don't see that at all. Lord, Deacon Foreman, look at Sister Maud Taylor coming out of the pastor's study, now you know, in front of the whole congregation, too. I'm not squeezing you boys too tight?" Mr. Foreman began reading. She turned to Coin. "I hope you haven't forgotten our talking the other day. It's real important, now you know it is. And your mother is one of the finest women I know. One of the finest. You sure gots a good mother. You know what I'm saying, son?"

"Yes, Mrs. Quick." His mind was so full of knowing that he thought his hopping heart was going to hop right up into his mouth. Mrs. Quick patted his head and then leaned over to Deaconess Westerfield whose hump showed like a crooked fist above the seat ahead. Woody took two agates out of his pocket and played a modest game of marbles in the palm of his hand.

"Good morning, Deaconess Westerfield. Now you know it's hot as an oven in here. It's a wonder they don't open the windows. I'm glad Mrs. Jessup didn't try to make it . . . she's ailing you know. I hope they got her name on the Sick and Shut In List . . ."

Professor Meyers began to play the organ. Gradually the talking hum in the church became silence. Coin looked up at the senior choir in the loft, serious in their black robes but funny in the flat-topped hats with tassels. His eyes wandered to the lettering in gold on the wall over the organ pipes: HITHERTO HATH THE LORD HELPED US. He had read it many times before but now he wanted to know what "hitherto" was. After his unsuccessful game of marbles, Woody was gazing at Deacon Loring squeezed in the big chair below the pulpit.

"How they gonna get his casket out of the church when he dies? He's bigger than the doorway."

Coin wasn't listening; the baptismal pool fascinated him this morning like it never had before. The water painted on the curved wall behind Reverend Brooks's chair was filled with a strange lemon-colored light. Christ was walking through the light, walking on water while silver fishes underneath swam around his toes looking straight out at Coin with hard eyes like Woody's purple aggies.

When the organ music had died down there was only the sound of Undertaker Ward's fans snapping back and forth until Reverend Brooks entered the auditorium from his study and stood at the pulpit.

"We begin our services this morning with the singing of hymn number 322: *How Firm a Foundation*."

He nodded to Professor Meyers, stretched his arms wide, as the organ announced the theme. The congregation arose. Mr. Foreman passed a hymnal to Woody who passed it to Coin. Mrs. Quick didn't need a book. She knew all hymns by heart. Her voice dominated the amen corner. Her body moved up and down emphasizing the rhythm with such force that the floor shook. Her mouth opened so wide once a fly was almost imprisoned behind gold teeth.

How firm a foundation ye saints of the Lord
Is laid for your faith by His excellent word.

Instead of just singing the regular words Woody made up his own and, although Coin laughed in his throat, he kept a straight face.

When Abie and Woody were playing red rover.
Coin gave Esther a four leaf clover.

Mr. Foreman had closed his eyes and was singing blind. Sister Westerfield's hump rocked so close sometimes Coin was tempted to touch it. He wouldn't get back to the baptismal pool until after the hymn was over. Sister Dora Highsmith, next to Deaconess Westerfield, didn't sing at all. She just uttered yes, yes, yesses at regular intervals as if her mouth were filled with gravy she couldn't swallow or else just wanted to hold the taste in her mouth. Bernice's high, sweet voice had no fooling in it this morning. When they sat down Mrs. Quick put her whole behind way back in the pew. Coin had to sit on edge. She smelled of Argo starch. He hoped Woody wouldn't start any stuff with that hump because Mrs. Quick had an eagle eye like Mama. Sharper maybe.

Deacon Loring struggled out of his chair to read the notices. His voice was like a bass drum. "On this Monday evening at eight o'clock, the Willing Workers Society will join with the Dorcas Society at the home of Mrs. Elba Fuller to discuss plans for raising funds for our pastor's twenty-fifth anniversary. . . . On Tuesday evening in the Sunday school room the Society of the Sons of Virginia will meet with Deacon Foreman, President . . . in the Sunday school par . . ."

Coin glanced at his father out of the corner of his eye and was proud that he was president and had his name read out in church. If Mama was here she'd be proud of him too. He wondered why Mrs. Quick kept gazing at his father. She looked and looked. Sitting on the edge of the seat, he put his nose practically under Deaconess Westerfield's hump. He studied the shape and wondered what it looked like underneath her clothes. Then he felt ashamed to think anything like that and turned away. But his face met Mrs. Quick's bosom and she patted his head. He turned the other way and Woody was slumped down in sleep. The drum beat and beat and he noticed that the rhythm of it matched the jerking rhythm of his heart. It was the sick and shut in notice.

"Sister Rosetta Sylvester, 478 Hancock Street, thanks all her friends who have prayed for her and sent flowers. She hopes to be able to attend services soon with the help of God. Mr. Albert Zeno died at his home at twenty-three minutes past five o'clock this morning. He had been ailing for some time. Funeral services to be announ . . ." A slight murmur curled through the church.

"He had the ulcer of the brain," Deaconess Westerfield leaned backwards to hiss.

"Abscess, Deaconess, abscess of the brain," Mrs. Quick hissed right back.

He remembered Mr. Zeno and couldn't think of him dead. He still wore his Civil War uniform and Coin knew there couldn't be a Memorial or Sunday school anniversary parade without him at the head carrying the torn flag and spry as a grasshopper even if they did say he was over eighty years old. He'd be there waving the flag to the sidewalk people just as large as life. Even if he wasn't there, he'd be there. No. The dead part didn't bother him. It was the sick part. Sicknesses he'd never heard of and they must somehow be connected with his mother. All sick was part of his present life and he had no time to lose if he was going to pray. He'd go up this minute, if he could, but the doors of the church hadn't been opened. Next was the sermon. That would take longer than he could bear. And all the amens and people falling out. Then the collection. Begging by Reverend Brooks for every kind of reason. They'd take two or three of them. He'd have to wait through more maybe before they opened the doors for "new members, Christians, children who were worthy to pray to God," Popa said.

". . . the collection for last Sunday was four hundred and twenty-six dollars and fifty-three cents. The pastor hopes we can bring it up to five hundred this Sunday. No sacrifice is too great to carry forward the Lord's work."

"You know they didn't even utter Mrs. Jessup's name."

"List of Tithers: Mrs. Marguerite Curley, Mrs. Lorraine Jackson, Deacon Amos Moon, Miss Lucille Spence, Mrs. Effie Weaver, Miss Jeanne English . . ."

After the notices the senior choir rose to sing the anthem: *How Beautiful Are Thy Dwelling Places, Oh Lord*. Coin knew he couldn't sit on edge much longer. His behind was getting numb-er and numb-er. He didn't want to listen to the hissing voices and his mother was alone at home waiting at the window. He asked his father if he could go to the back of the church. Coin squirmed past Mrs. Quick's knees. When he was standing in a clear space under former Pastor Seward's in stained glass, he wondered if his elbow had touched the wood of the pew as he passed Mrs. Quick, or the hump of Deaconess Westerfield.

". . . and if there be any among you who wishes to declare before God and this gathering his intention to follow the ways of the Lord and His Son who said, 'Come unto me all you who are weary and heavy laden and I will give you rest,' and again, 'Suffer little children to come unto me for of such is the Kingdom of Heaven,' for all those who have not yet been saved and desire the fullness of life in our Lord, I declare the doors of this church open for membership."

The organ whispered the first few bars of, *There Is a Fountain Filled with Blood*, while Reverend Brooks outstretched his arms. He must know what Coin had decided to do for each word was a special invitation and a plea. The choir, now standing, sang full force, their singing before the organ swooped down the aisle and surrounded Coin like a wind drawing his feet to the mourners' bench:

> *There is a fountain filled with blood*
> *Drawn from Emanuel's veins,*
> *And sinners plunge beneath the flood,*
> *Lose all their guilty sta . . . . aiiiins,*
> *Lose all their guilty stains.*

But he couldn't move. Maybe Woody would go up, or Bernice, or anybody before him and he would follow. Even though Reverend Brooks pleaded in a voice, as soothing as sunshine, over the music, "Won't you come, won't you, or YOU or YOU . . ." nobody went up. The choir sang the second verse more quietly:

> *The dying thief rejoiced to see*
> *That fountain in his day . . .*

The light from the stained-glass window threw faint blue color on Coin's hands. He felt his mother. The whole church was humming to the singing:

> *And there may I, though vile as he,*
> *Wash all my sins away.*
> *Wash all my sins awawwwwaay,*
> *Wash all my sins awa . . .*

The humming was in his toes, it surrounded the beating of his heart, it was on his head like a rubber swimming cap, close, tight. The hands of Reverend Brooks still called to him. The singing had stopped and only the timid patting of feet in unison building to a tramp, tramping, for him to lay his life down. He took a step forward and Reverend Brooks must have seen the movement. The voice was a magnet now that victory was in sight.

"Won't you come, won't you give your life to him. Suffer who to come unto me? 'Suffer little children to come unto me for of . . . for of SUCH, I say, is the Kingdom of Heaven.' Won't you come? It's an easy walk. An easy walk because the path is clear . . . clear . . . clear. It's a short walk. An easy walk unto His Kingdom. . . ."

An easy walk past his father and Woody and Mrs. Quick? What would Bernice say? Would PeeWee Taylor laugh? An easy walk between all the faces?

". . . It's a way strewn with palm branches, it's the way He trod for us . . ." He didn't care who trod it. He couldn't go, not up there by himself. The aisle had become half a mile long . . . as far as to Blake Avenue. The pulpit was a pin dot, all the choir tassels swayed and blurred together . . . he couldn't go.

The music, the tramping, the voice of Reverend Brooks had stopped; there was a silence like in the cellar sometimes. When Coin found his father's face and heard what he remembered from the dark . . . "the boys heard Mrs. Quick, Popa . . ." light was on his father's forehead. They looked at each other over the distance of last night. In that silence, Coin began his walk down the center aisle. Heads turned as they heard the squeak, squeak of his shoes, he felt air rushing to his heel. He was blind, he was set in motion and there was no turning back. He was a soft ball rolling slowly in the middle of an empty street.

He was there sitting on the mourners' bench looking up at Reverend Brooks behind the pulpit smiling down at him as if his martyrdom had saved the sinning world he preached about in his sermon. He was bigger than the monument in Prospect Park, he looked bigger than a tree. Coin was scared and voices flew around him like leaves.

"Bless his little heart."

"Deacon Foreman must be proud."

"His youngest son. It just touches my heart to see a little soldier like that."

"Jesus' little lamb, Jesus' lamb." He was alone in a pit. The congregation stood on all sides singing the closing hymn:

> Blest be the tie that binds
> Our hearts in Christian love,
> The fellowship the . . .

The collected voices rolled, bursting out of the wind that had surrounded him before. His body let out a cold sweat, his teeth began to clack.

The ceiling in the deacons' room was low, pressing down. Deacon Loring and his father, Deaconesses Redmond and Westerfield sat in a semicircle before him. He felt like in the movies, the cops and robbers and the third degree, until his father told him that he was mighty proud of what he'd done.

"We're all proud," beamed Deaconess Westerfield, "he's come like Christ to the temple while yet a child."

"Does he know what he's doing, that's the thing," said Deaconess Redmond shooting what Coin interpreted as an I'll-get-even-with-you look at his father. Mr. Foreman cleared his throat.

"I think he can answer all the necessary questions. Are you ready, son?" Coin didn't recognize his own voice replying, "Yes, sir."

"I know he's ready," Deaconess Westerfield hissed quietly at Deaconess Redmond. "Would you like to put the first question, Sister?"

If Woody were here he'd answer that old Deaconess Redmond, or Bernice. Bernice would let her have it better than this morning, but momentary courage gained in imagining how they would have acted failed him as the first question was put.

"Who made you?" Everything left Coin's mind. Why don't they open up a window? Mr. Foreman cleared his throat again and smiled encouragement. Coin just couldn't think.

"That's not hard, son."

"I wish you'd let the boy answer for himself," Deaconess Redmond snapped. "I put the first question a second time." And she leaned over him with that dandelion smell. Coin knew it came out of the peppery black wart on her nose. "Who made you?"

"Dr. Henry."

Deaconess Redmond began to laugh in triumph right at his father. "Nowadays children of some folks get their raising in the streets." Mr. Foreman's mustache bristled. Coin felt sorry for his father who answered weakly, "That's not Christian, Deaconess."

"Not Christian either to chase me out of my appointed place. Not Christian; why that little hussy of a Bernice . . ."

"Sister, Sister," intoned Deacon Loring, then turning to Coin, "think hard son, who made you?"

Coin thought hard and finally whispered, "God made me."

"Of course if you're going to give the child all the answers . . ." Deaconess Redmond had opened her mouth but Deaconess Westerfield put her voice right into it.

"Where is Heaven, son?"

Coin could answer that all right. "Up past the clouds and God's peeking down."

"Hark now to this boy," was a joyful sound from Deaconess Westerfield.

If he could just touch that hump, he bet he could answer any question from A to Z.

"My God doesn't need to peek," Deaconess Redmond flared out her nose. The wart got darker.

"Sister," Deacon Loring said, "if you talk like this before a little child, in an important and troubling time . . . for God's sake use your common sense." Coin didn't like them. They were worse than in P.S. 64 when Miss Binatree got mad with the principal in the auditorium. He didn't care now. The going-up feeling was gone. He wanted to talk to Woody, he wanted to . . .

"What is your favorite Bible story?" Deacon Loring asked kindly. That was easy. His father had told him so many all he had to do was pick. He didn't care if they liked it or not.

"Shadrach, Meshach and Abednego."

"That's a fine story, son. I forget what it's all about for the moment."

"About a furnace and fire. They said that the Lord would keep him from getting burnt up so it didn't make a bit of difference if the king put them in, they didn't care . . ."

His father's face looked proud of him, even Deaconess Redmond was listening.

". . . so that old Nebuchadnez put them in to burn into a crisp. They did their praying inside and the Lord he sent an angel with wings spreading out to keep the fire from burning up their clothes and their eyes. Nebuchadnez sent for the fireman who had on a red helmet and asked, 'They all burned to a crisp?' The fireman took a long look and guess what? They was sitting down in the middle of the fire playing mumblety peg with a pocket knife."

Everybody was just smiling.

". . . then Nebuchadnez began to tremble like he was a crazy lunatic; he opened and let them out. They was cool as cucumbers. They didn't have their knife though, the angel had taken that away so he could teach the other angels to play mumblety peg on their day off."

He finished and moved in his seat with satisfaction, looking from one face to another. He knew Deaconess

Redmond had something up her sleeve and now she was taking it out. "Why do you pray, Coin Foreman?" He had his answer ready because that was why he was here. "To ask God for something and get it."

"That seems to be just about the gist of it," Deaconess Westerfield said. Every one laughed but his father. Mr. Foreman drew his chair close to his son's.

"Did you feel anything different when you decided to give your life to the Lord? Did you see anything?"

"I saw the little man."

"What was he like, son?"

They all held their breath.

"He was made out of sunshine right behind Mama."

The questioners exchanged glances and Coin thought that they didn't believe him at all.

"But I did see him, I did. I saw him just as plain." If they didn't believe he wouldn't be admitted and he did see him, he did, he did. A tear rolled down his cheek and went into his mouth.

"We know you saw him, bless your little heart. You're one of the anointed." Heads nodded seriously. Even Deaconess Redmond looked at him in a kind of wonder.

"Did he speak to you, son?"

"He didn't say nothing, Deaconess Westerfield. He was just there and when I looked again he was gone."

"The spirit of God has made itself manifest unto you," Deacon Loring whispered. Coin was surprised that the bass drum in his voice could get so soft. He felt holy. The spirit of God was made manifest to Him.

"Kneel down, son."

They all knelt. Deacon Loring was a black hill by Coin's side. Mr. Foreman began to pray.

"Dear heavenly Father, another soul is offered up to Thy service. A young soul. A child's. Keep him. Protect him. Let him grow in spirit as well as in body . . ."

There were three amens.

". . . we know that the way is not easy. We seek light in darkness, a heaven of sweetness, after the trials and tribulations of this sour earth. We go on struggling; we go on seeking. We pass on Thy word to our children somehow . . ."

All his father said was connected with his mother's affliction, with Mrs. Carth's word, with Esther's freckles. It was connected with the ink and stars he couldn't find in Popa's sky.

". . . and now this child, this tender child, has decided of himself to give his life to Thee. Grant that in the years to come he will find comfort in this hour; grant that he will find that comfort in Thee which removes mountains and causes the seas to part; comfort that will make his life a rich vessel when robbers of time and shakers of dust come to his heart."

His father's voice had no roar in it. It wasn't the blessing tone, or the wide momps-where's-the-napkin voice. This voice was calm and loving and sad like his mother's face. He had never heard it before. It hurt like her arm and leg. It was Popa's voice but Mama was by its side. Mama was in this room. He was dedicated.

". . . grant him a measure of success in all his undertakings, grant that this morning will serve as an example to other children who have not yet found it in their hearts to lay down their lives upon the altar of truth and faith in Thee, as this boy Coin Foreman, nine years old, but a seer in the service of Thy Son. Bless this precious hour and all that take part in the holy minutes of it. Until Thy great glory, Lord, amen."

They stood around him beaming. His father shook his hand. Deacon Loring squeezed his arm. Deaconess Redmond patted his head. She sure had a heavy pat. And last of all, Deaconess Westerfield, who had waited her turn, threw her arms about him.

"Oh Jesus, ain't he sweet. I'm just crazy about this little lamb."

Coin felt brave and secure as Woody, as his hands, returning her embrace, reached for the hump.

From the baptismal pool Coin couldn't make out any shapes but the lighted candles in mid-air, arranged around the rostrum. When Mr. Foreman saw them earlier that evening, he declared that Reverend Brooks was introducing pagan practices into the Baptist church. Coin was too busy getting into his long white robe, in the deacons' room, to worry about his father's criticism. He was going to be washed in the blood of the lamb. Deaconess Westerfield called the water in the pool blood. Woody said it wasn't any different from bathtub water. It wasn't blood but it was different though. He was standing right in it in front of Reverend Brooks who had on his black gown and rubber boots. The water was warm for one thing and it was dark blue, blue like when his mother dipped Blu-In in washing water and it had smell of iodine . . . the holy smell. The tiny waves of real water licked against the painted fishes.

Reverend Brooks stretched up his right hand and chanted to Coin loud enough for everybody to hear, "I baptize thee in the name of the Father and of the Son and of the Holy Ghost," whispered, "hold your nose, boy," and ended with a long, "amen." Amens came from the church too.

Coin was thrust into the water and came up hollering just like Deaconess Westerfield told him every Christian did when he was transformed. As he walked dripping up the ramp leading to the deacons' room from the pool, he heard the triumphant singing of the congregation:

> *Hallelujah, it's done,*
> *I believe on the Son,*
> *I am saved by the blood*
> *Of the crucified One.*

The song came toward him like going up steps to a door. The way was opened for him to ask the Lord to help his mother. And so in his flannel robe, shivering, with the music mounting in his wet flesh, he got down on his knees . . . and began to cry. That was the way Mr. Foreman found him.

Coin thought that the candlelight would hide his crying eyes but when he opened the door that led to the church the brightness startled him, faces turned toward him, voices popped around him like rice crispies in the warm milky light. He stopped and looked for his father who was standing next to Deaconess Westerfield looking at his watch. Woody was grinning at him with a Halloween face and Bernice concentrated on the ceiling. There was a hump in Coin's hand, uncovered, and he felt the gristle flesh. He wouldn't even glance at Deaconess Westerfield. The stained-glass window stared dead with no sunshine. Converts from three Sundays back stood embarrassed at the mourners' bench where he was alone last Sunday. The black hill, Deacon Loring, moved toward him and shook his hand. His right hand of fellowship was tight as a wooden vise. Old Sisters rushed up and hugged him in their arms. They all smelled like dandelions. (If you pick a dandelion, you'll piss in the bed.) Someone thrust a bar of melting chocolate into his hand. Sweet and damp. Then his father came up.

"Don't shake my hand, Popa."

"The right hand of fellowship, son. The Christian . . . wipe your hand. Wipe that candy off your hand . . ."

"Welcome," chanted Reverend Brooks.

Woody ran up. "Kiss your hand, brother Jesus." Bernice laughed and gritted her teeth in the sound he didn't like. He felt the Blu-In water in his throat. "Shake your hand, brother," came from dark-blue suits with badges swinging from lapels. "Ain't he the sweetest though." "Christ in the temple." "Sweet lamb, sweet, brown lamb." "Jesus' little lambs, Jesus' lamb." "Hallelujah, it's done." "Lord have mercy, he's saved, he's washed and concentrated." The voices mounted.

He gazed at the naked electric bulbs above, until they became bright blue and orange. When he looked away spots were in front of him; each face that met his eyes was only spots. The whole church was running to and fro shaking hands. The converts that stood so still were shaking hands, fast as playing the piano. His mother's face was a spot. A black spot on the rug. When will he see right again? Could he ever pray for her? He thought it would be easy after the water. But when he had tried to pray, he only felt the flat pat of Deaconess Redmond on his head and he was nervous in between his legs. That was when Popa came in to the deacons' room and he had to dress without going to the bathroom. Although no organ played, there was a singing. Mrs. Quick's voice rose up like the fireman's siren marking twelve o'clock in school. She was by his side holding his waist, singing, singing Argo starch into the air. The congregation began too. Standing and sitting, high and low. Singing for Coin, bending down, singing in the half of a conversation, singing through chewing gum. Reverend Brooks was chewing gum. Spearmint gum. Spearmint singing. Mrs. Quick counted his ribs in rhythm:

> *I come to the garden alone,*
> *While the dew is still on the roses;*
> *And the voice I hear,*
> *Falling on my ear;*

The Son of God discloses.
And He walks with me and He talks with me,
And He tells me I am His own,
And the joy we share as we tarry there,
None other has ever known.

"Yes, yes, yes, yes, yes, yes, yesssssssss, yes, yes," gobbled Sister Dora Highsmith, "yes, yes, yes." He knew his right hand was numb. Numb from all the grips and the wringing. Lick the chocolate offa my hand. His face was in the pillow of Mrs. Quick's bosom. It rose and fell with the beats of the song. His teeth bit the black cloth of her dress and he tasted dye. "Rest your head there and pray for your mother. Rest your head," her voice was giggling and he tickled some more with his nose right where the big mounds curved into a valley.

At his first communion the following Sunday he felt calmer than he had at the right hand of fellowship or the baptism, for that matter. The board of deacons and deaconesses were standing formal in a semicircle in front of their pews, from aisle to aisle, waiting to deliver Christ's body and blood to the congregation. The white dresses of the deaconesses shone bright but there were no faces above them and the deacons, in dark blue, disappeared altogether. Warm wind from the windows on either side of the church blew the candles to flickering and almost out. Sometimes the whole scene was changed and Coin thought Jesus had something to do with it because they were breaking His body and flowing His blood. But when he got used to the quick changes, the flickering and the dim, he felt more comfortable than in daytime church. He was led to a special bench, before the collection table with the other converts, where Reverend Brooks was breaking a loaf of "unleavened bread without yeast" (Deaconess Westerfield described it). He held it high in one hand and broke with the other. White birds in candlelight fell from his hand onto silver ground. Organ music was their singing. Spread before him, too, were glasses no bigger than a thumb with a dark-red juice in them. They were standing in holes on a silver plate to keep them from sliding around. Reverend Brooks held the bread plate up high as his arms could reach. The black robe went out from his sides like bat wings outlined with candlelight. Coin gazed up on high. Two deacons received the plates with the broken bread and began to pass it out. Deacon Loring's head leaned over him huge and drops of sweat settled on the piece Coin took. Reverend Brooks returned to the pulpit and the candles thrust his shadow against the back wall, his neck was in the baptismal pool. The shadow was Lon Chaney in *The Unholy Three*.

Reverend Brooks delivered the words, "Jesus took bread and blessed it, and brake it, and gave it to the disciples, and said, take, eat; this is my body." Coin didn't want to, because his piece had Deacon Loring's sweat in it. His father was looking at him and he put the bread in his mouth, tried to swallow but it stayed like a lump in his mouth.

The deacons were passing out the grape juice. Coin

wanted some. He couldn't swallow with the lump of unleavened bread, moistened by Deacon Loring, in his mouth. He reached very carefully for a glass and held it firmly in one hand. While Reverend Brooks said the other words he bowed his head like everybody else, only he raised his free hand to his mouth and poked the bread into his palm.

"For this is my blood of the new testament which is shed for many for the remission of sins. . . ."

Coin quickly thrust the soft slimy dough into his pocket and then drank with the congregation and Reverend Brooks the blood Christ had shed for him.

It was all over now. He was a real Christian from head to foot, inside and out. And as he sat celebrating with Bernice and Woody and his father in Undertaker Ward's Confectionery Shop, eating a big frappe of strawberry sherbert, whipped cream, walnuts, crushed pineapple and cherries, he was preparing for miracles.

I T WOULD be a holiday that night for all Berriman Street. There'd be something else, too, to make the joy double, so Coin woke up that morning talking pig latin.

"Oodgay orningmay, Ammay, oodgay orningmay Oodway, oodgay ormingay ethay orldway," he chanted dashing to the front window to see what was happening outside. "Good morning, the world!" he shouted, forgetting the pig latin. The block was practically empty except for Mrs. Schneider polishing her windows. The trees sparkled as if the sunlight were tinsel on them.

Little bumpy streams played in each gutter. The street had been washed already. Coin looked up and down. He opened the window, poked his head out and with a fist traced his mother's name in the air: NAOMI STARR FOREMAN. There was a smell of mint. Someone was making candy for tonight. Coin sang across to Mrs. Schneider.

"Abie up yet?"

"Nu. Abie, he's gone to market already."

"Tell him to come over when he gets back, huh? We're going for firewood."

"I tell him."

If she polishes that old window any more, she'll wear the glass out.

"How is your Mama?"

"Mama's fine. How's yours?" Coin knew that Abie's grandmother was dead but asked the question all the same. Mrs. Schneider stopped and waved the rag at him with mock anger, tossing her head from side to side. Then she turned to the Carth house next door and said something about Mrs. Carth was poisoning the children on the block. Coin smelled dog doo peanuts and closed the window. A fly was on the pane in the right-hand corner, with a jacket of sun on, cleaning its face with teeny wire legs, flying wings tucked in. The eyes were drops of shiny purple. Coin watched for a moment, then rapped on the glass. The fly let out its wings and flew to the opposite corner. Coin rapped there. It flew to the middle. Coin rapped again.

The fly kept settling to clean its face. That fly wouldn't budge again for anything.

Back at the bed he shook Woody. "Etgay uplay azylay onesbay."

"Aah shat ap," Woody mumbled, pulling the covers over his head and pretending to snore.

"Ebay uickqay Iay mellsay reakfastbay."

"Ervesay reakfastbay otay emay inay edbay," answered Woody popping his head out. The smile was red and sleepy at the same time.

Mrs. Foreman stood at the door to the bedroom. "You boys hurry up and dress. And stop that street talk."

"It's not street talk," defended Woody, "it's pig latin and it's official."

"I'll official you both if you don't wash and eat this farina before it gets cold and lumpy."

"I don't want no lumpy."

"Where's everybody?" asked Coin cocking his head and smiling at Mrs. Foreman. It was the first time he had really seen her today and as he began rubbing the sleep out of his eyes he suddenly saw her running to the stove, lifting a big pot of boiling clothes with both her hands, washing them and all the suds up to her elbow in foam of breaking pretty bubbles. She was humming a song she learned when she was a child:

> *Call that possum,*
> *Call that possum.*

She wrang out sheets and winter underwear. Her thin black hair was filled with drops of water. Hanging out the clothes and later taking in the stiff forms like snowmen out of petticoats and bloomers piled on the tubs and icebox and in baskets on the floor. Then the stiffness went out of them, because of the heat, and they sagged to damp lumps. Late into the night came the ironing. The hungry night. He woke up so hungry and: "Mama, I'm hungry."

"You had your dinner, child."

"Wasn't enough."

"I can't sleep."

She took the last caramel out of a bag and he went back to bed with a sweet taste inside him. Woody went in. "Mama, I'm hungry." Coin knew the bag was empty.

"Mama, I'm hungry."

"There's nothing left."

"Coin's got a candy."

"Go back to bed."

"Coin's got some; you gimmie some."

Woody got a smack and through the door he saw his mother ironing. There was a big pile still to do.

He was frightened when he looked now with his hands away from his eyes; she was dragging the leg. She had never done all that. She had been sick since he was born and how could he have seen all that carrying on? He made her sick when he was born. He was responsible, but how?

"Woody, don't you kick me under the table again. If you do I'll scalp you with the hatchet and hang your skull on the drum in Chris's house."

"I didn't kick you, dumbell."

He wished it were tonight.

> *Call that possum*
> *Take him to your heart.*

"Woody, I didn't mean nothing."

"Everybody's getting prepared for the block party tonight and you children batting words around. Be sure to bring enough wood for the fire. Put it in the lot next to Mrs. Jeffers."

"Woody, the woodman," said Coin.

"Coin, the christoin."

"When's Mrs. Quick coming, Mama?"

"In plenty good time. Around six, I expect."

"Aw, Mama, are you gonna miss the block party?" asked Woody with the hatchet in his hand, testing the blade to see how sharp it was or wasn't. "I bet you won't have any fun at that old Miracle Church."

"Don't you worry about me. Mrs. Quick will be mighty disappointed if I don't go; she's had her heart set on it for weeks and this is the last session for the summer."

She spoke about it as if it wasn't the most important night in the world. Anyway it didn't matter. Mrs. Quick was sure to be johnny-on-the spot.

"Woody, don't gobble your cereal."

"Oay akay, Ammay."

Even Agnes said Mama should go to prove something or other to him. He hadn't heard what something was but Agnes must believe and she didn't very often. It would be all right. Coin hurried with his farina. The faster he went, the faster the day would go. And he had prayed for more than a half hour last night. That was something good. And he had another idea too to make double sure.

"Ethay astlay ownday siay umbay," cried Woody, grabbing the hatchet and crashing down the stairs, letting it bump on each step.

"Woody, everything's gonna be all right when Mama gets home tonight."

"You sure?"

"Sure."

"You?"

"Nope!"

On the way to the vacant lots beyond Dumont Avenue Woody began skipping and singing with Abie accompanying him on a kazoo:

> *Three blind mice,*
> *They got lice*
> *In their eyes*
> *By surprise*
> *Ain't that nize. . . .*

The song made Coin remember his blind time. It was so clear that he stopped short. Abie and Woody seemed to disappear into the heat that waved up from the sidewalk; the houses swayed and the street sounds went far away like whispering—peddlers yelling about vegetables for sale, cabbages and grapes, I got bananas, goody bananas for sale. The trucks ran on cotton streets and no auto horns honked. A dog chased a cat but he didn't hear no fighting sounds. He sat down on the curb and put his hands to his eyes. His head felt hot and as he rubbed his eyeballs splintered light shot in front of him. He felt like he was in Miss Horwitz' house that time when Woody had scarlet fever and he couldn't stay in the low-down bed at home. So for a week he stayed with Miss Horwitz. There was the big bed all to himself. He missed Woody's warmth and even the kicking. One night it just happened. He had opened his eyes and there was nothing. No shadows creeping on the walls to frighten him, no light from the windows, no pictures catching the street lamp. He held his hands up but he couldn't see them. He stared at each wall: only solid and thick. He began to sweat. The sweat rolled down his cheeks as thick as buttermilk. Was his sweat black like everything now? He held his eyelids wide till he felt the balls popping. Then closed his eyes again and opened them. It was the same. Only blacker. He yelled. He couldn't help it. The sound came out of his thighs because they burned. He gasped out, "Miss Horwitz, Miss Horwitzzzzzzzzzz!"

He was blind. He knew it. He was in midnight that would never be morning. He wouldn't ever see nothing again. There was a flap, flap sound. Flap, flap, psffffff. Flap, flap, flap. Bats had come for him.

Flap, flap all over his face. Flap, flap nearer and nearer and something hugged him. He began to fight.

"No, no, no. I didn't do nothing, no. Mamaaaaaaaa." Something stank a little bit like rotting potatoes. Stank warm. Suddenly light was all around. He was caught in the middle of an electric bulb and he saw through glass that Miss Horwitz was there. Her face was close and wrinkled like when you blew on coffee.

"What frightened you? What frightened you, little boy?" She was smiling like Miss Raidin when she was mad, and pieces of sleep were in the corners of her eyes.

"Nothing."

"Nothing and you yelling me out of a night's sleep."

"I thought . . . I thought I was blind, Miss Horwitz, I couldn't see a thing. I thought I was blind for good like Cousin Troy Starr."

Then Miss Horwitz began to laugh. She shook all over with laughing as if what he said wound her up like Popa's alarm clock. She'd ring forever.

"You're a big baby. Go on back to sleep."

He didn't sleep for a long time after he heard her mules go flap, flap, flap back to the other room. After a while he heard her tip back and open the thick draperies.

> *Does your mother know you're out*
> *With your tommy sticking out.*

He didn't see Chris O'Connor come up chanting.

"Where's Woody and Abie?"

"Near the nanny goat lady's shack."

"Com' on then."

"Okay."

They walked idly toward the lots and he thought about tonight after his mother got home: how it would be if the block party lasted long enough she'd dance in the streets, maybe, like Mr. Jeffers. Oh boy. He'd never be a baby again. He had been fooled once at Miss Horwitz'.

He and Chris zipped up to Woody and Abie who had already found a limb of a poplar tree. Coin had gotten it all straightened out. He sang one of Woody's rimes:

> *There's a soldier in the grass*
> *With a bullet up his ass.*

The four of them shouted the chorus while Woody kept time with the hatchet:

> *Take it out, take it out, take it out.*

At six o'clock sharp Mrs. Quick hopped around the corner at Berriman and Sutter, wearing chicken colors. She skipped right into the midst of waiting children. Her straw hat, with the feather, bobbed greetings to right and left. Woody whispered to Coin that she looked just like a Rhode Island red hen but Coin was too excited by what her punctual appearance meant to see any fun.

"Hello, Mrs. Quick," smiled Woody and was first in line behind her.

"Why bless you, child, your face looks just as spry as a jaybird on the wing."

"Good evening, Mrs. Quick," intoned Abie dancing into place after Woody. Then came Chris O'Connor on his green scooter that went faster than Abie's but he wouldn't race Abie. Then Leslie and Teddie Esterbrook and Abigail Bernstein and Charlie Richardson. Her name sounded like a magpie bird the way Mrs. Quick said it.

"Why Abigail, you're just the cleanest child on the block."

She hadn't seen Abigail that day Chris threw mud all over her pink ribbons and she cried like she'd never stop raining. Esther joined last so as to be close to Coin.

Esther said, "Mrs. Quick, Coin's waiting for you."

"I know that, honey. I seen him first thing." She brushed a fly off her brown taffeta bosom.

The musicians the whole block had chipped in to hire were coming from Blake Avenue. The kids broke rank and ran like sparrows toward the uniformed men. Coin was glad to be alone with Mrs. Quick at last.

"How's it gonna be, Mrs. Quick?"

"Why, I believe it's gonna be just fine. I had a good dream last night and you know about them dreams."

"I prayed a long time."

"That's the spirit."

"What does he do? First, I mean."

"Why son, he preaches first."

"About what?"

"I do hope it's gonna be *Dry Bones in the Valley*. I do love to see Reverend S. Robert Blanton shinney up the pole."

"Like a monkey."

"Well," she laughed, "he's too old for monkey business," winking down at Coin. Coin winked back like he understood.

"And then what else?"

"Why then he concentrates the dimes."

"What's that?"

"Why son, each one holds up his dime for collections and it's blessed to the service of the Lord."

"Yes?" He wanted to hear the best part.

"Then each one that wants the miracle holds up a dollar or more, look at Mrs. Jeffers switching herself down the street, and that's blessed."

"Yes?"

"Then the needy brings up their affliction and they kneels down and he prays for each and every one separate and they think real deep on the Lord. Many rise up well and cured."

"Is Mama . . . ?"

"Your mother's got the strength and faith to remove the mountains."

"Nothing's gonna be hard?"

"If you believe on the Lord. And you know he's in our corner."

"Yes," said Coin. He was satisfied by the time they entered the Foreman dining room.

"Why Mrs. Foreman, you look like the miracle done taken place already."

Mrs. Foreman looked at Coin.

"I wouldn't say that, Mrs. Quick. I'm going for the outing. I haven't been over to the Bronx in almost three years."

"Well now, that purple certainly does become you. I wish Mrs. Jessup could see you now. I wish she could clap her eyes on that black straw hat. And against your gray hair, too. She always holds that gray and black are the only colors. I adds purple to the list."

Coin went into the bedroom and came out immediately with something behind his back.

"Mama," he said quietly, "here's a flower for your dress." He handed her a crepe paper rose about the size of a dinner plate. His mother looked at it and smiled. He knew it was all right.

"Aren't you gonna put it on?"

"Of course I'm going to wear it, son." She tucked it into the bosom of her dress.

"That's the handsomest rose I ever seen," admired Mrs. Quick, "just the prettiest that ever grew."

"Oh, it ain't real," Coin said shyly, wishing it were.

"You put a real rose alongside it and I defy you to tell me which is which."

Coin looked up at his mother who said quickly, "It's six in one hand and half a dozen in the other."

The room looked different with his mother all dressed up in it. She was another picture. She was the one of all.

"Are you ready now, Mrs. Foreman?"

"Just about. I want to say goodbye to Popa. He's in the back yard with his crops." She leaned out the window and called, "Goodbye, Popa. Be a good chairman tonight."

Coin and Mrs. Quick stood at the other window as Mr. Foreman's voice rang up.

"Momps, you going now, Momps?"

"Yes."

"Take good care of my girl, Mrs. Quick. Enjoy the service, Momps," then his voice got a frown on it. "What in the world is that on your dress?"

"Coin gave me a rose. I think he made it himself."

"This boy's just as thoughtful," Mrs. Quick called. "You've got a gardenful there, Deacon."

"Yes, I can raise a whole meal right in this back yard. All except the meat and poultry, of course."

"Well, Deacon, they's plenty of spring chickens flying around loose these days." Mrs. Quick's bosom shook with laughter.

Mrs. Foreman stroked her arm, smiling down at Popa.

"Goodbye, Popa," and she threw him the crepe paper rose before she faced Mrs. Quick. Coin watched the rose go down.

"Oh, I'm sorry son, I didn't think."

"That's all right, Mama."

"Mr. Foreman sure remind me of down home working in the cotton. I thought I'd melt away picking cotton, straighten your hat a little to the left, and just picking. The sun sometimes shot up to one hundred twenty degrees."

"We'd better be going, Mrs. Quick, or we won't get a seat."

Coin went to the station with them and watched

the big purple bow on Mrs. Quick's behind wave howdydo as she went. Mrs. Foreman moved up the steps one at a time. He stood at the bottom landing until the train roared out toward the happy ending planned for tonight.

"Coin, what are you doing up there!" He had climbed to the closet over the tubs where Bernice used to bathe him and Woody on Saturday nights, and was reaching for the bottle of grape juice.

"Answer me, Coin, what are you doing up there," Agnes' voice hit him like a spitball. Miss Horwitz was standing near the stove with a glass of buttermilk in her hand. She'd turn to buttermilk one of these days.

"Communion."

"Communion, what?"

"To make double sure."

"Come down here and tell me what you're talking about."

"Yes, ma'am."

He climbed down carefully and stood in front of his sister.

"How many times have I told you not to say yes ma'am and no ma'am. When people speak to you call them by their name. Like yes Miss Horwitz or no Miss Horwitz. You're not in the cotton fields."

"Yes, Agnes."

What did ma'ams and sirs have to do with communion? And Miss Horwitz was beginning to laugh at him like the other time.

"Well?"

"I was going to take it for Mama. She left already." Agnes got real serious then. "Coin listen, listen, or you'll be very disappointed. Nothing's going to happen tonight. Mama's going to come back just the same. That's why she went, to prove that to you."

Agnes spoiled everything and now she was trying to spoil what he knew was going to happen. She was playing an April Fool on him in July.

Well, she could talk and talk like a record machine but he had seen the little man and all the deacons and deaconesses, and they were the holiest, said that when you prayed for something and believed hard you got it. Mama didn't play tricks. So when he looked at Agnes this time, he looked her straight in the eye.

"Mama believes it." He started to go.

"Coin."

"Nothing," answered Miss Horwitz for his sister. She turned to Agnes.

"He's old enough to take life the way it is, let him find out for himself. I had to and I wasn't much bigger than he is."

The block was like a big piece of candy, sweet in every part. Overhead loops of lights joined hands and everyone was filled with bright jewels like in the five and ten. They sparkled yellow and red and blue and green. They stretched from Blake Avenue to Sutter and the blocks beyond seemed tunnel-dark and dead. If you squinted they sent off sparks of their own color;

if you made your eyes wide, there was an extra glow and the colors faded into each other like the bands of a spinning top. The sky seemed so close he could pull it down like a window shade. He felt happy.

First the Jeffers lot for the weenies. Woody and Abie and Chris were already there. Mr. Jeffers was taking charge. Mrs. Jeffers stood back with the kids calling commands.

"No, no Cecil, let the blaze die down. Hot ashes are needed for weenies, not a blaze."

"Will you keep your big mouth shut, woman, I know how to work the damn thing."

But they weren't fussing. She laughed and he laughed when his eyes got full of smoke.

"Let me do it, Cecil. The way you carry on, it'll be three o'clock in the morning before the kids get supper."

Coin was crazy about Mrs. Jeffers because he knew that she'd see that they all got a plenty and to spare.

"Take the damn poker then, woman. I'll repair to better things inside." He pinched Coin's neck with a rough, kind hand as he passed.

"Don't go drinking it all now or they'll be nothing left for the others."

He liked Mr. Jeffers. Especially tonight. He was dressed up in his clothes from Trinidad; he matched the lights and merry. He was going in to drink and that's when he was best of all. He'd dance like everything and play like he was a little boy. Mrs. Jeffers had on a long skirt with all the colors and a waist that showed her shoulders. Her shoulders were nice. But best of all was the hat. Tall, it was white and stiff with two bows on top. They were birds and when she danced they'd fly. Fly white.

The kids had four weenies apiece, burnt and delicious with mustard and a roll. If they came back for more, nobody'd say: no-you-can't or don't-do-that or where-in-the-world-are-your-manners or there-isn't-any-more. They trooped to Mrs. Bernstein's stand for lemonade. They handed their cups to her again and she laughed with pleasure because for once there was enough. Abigail kept running into the house for more of this and that, and Coin imagined a big lemon tree in the Bernsteins' back yard and Abigail under it saying magic words for the lemons to grow and another magic word for them to drop down; she scooped up sugar from the ground and spices grew in the aireyway.

"Drink, drink," urged Mrs. Bernstein. The kids crowded around so that Esther couldn't get near the stand. Coin brought her a paper cup.

"Thank you, Coin."

Coin ran for another cup. Mrs. Schneider had the mint candy and fish, halavah cut the size of dominos, lemon drops, chocolate creams, peanuts in icing, and one package of Luden's cough drops.

The Kerkashners had the little sweet hot cakes in all shapes; stars and round, oblong and triangle, decorated with pink and blue and white icing.

The children rushed from one stand to the other stuffing themselves.

The ice cream cones were last. Esther's mother, Mrs. Polinski, served them and Esther handed them out to the hands that urged forward and forward. Dirty, joyous hands; happy, nervous fingers. Coin got a bigger one than anyone else and Esther promised him another one if he could eat it.

"Isn't this pleasant," Esther smiled; Coin thought of Miss Raidin handing him a report card with all good marks.

"It's the cat's meow," said Coin with ice cream streaming down his chin.

The band was tuning up for the first number. The sky had closed in dark and stars looked down. Coin thought of his mother, she must be kneeling now for the special time after the prayer, and Reverend S. Robert Blanton was saying "rise up and shake your affliction off." Mrs. Quick always referred to affliction. "Rise up and shake thy affliction off." There was a loud clash of cymbals. Coin danced over to the grandstand where the children were swaying hand in hand, smiling and blowing notes of their own noiselessly like water bubbles.

After the first band song, Mr. Foreman mounted the stand. A long streamer was caught on his arm and as he unwound it he said, "Looks like I'm trying to tear all the decorations down."

Everybody laughed and nudged each other. Coin loved to see his father this way, smiling and making fun out of any old thing that happened.

"Might be well if I just place this piece of red ribbon across my chest; some of you might take me for a foreign diplomat." The kids all clapped and Chris looked at Coin, taking his hand. "I bet he wished that was his father," Coin thought.

"Tonight, folks, is a celebration. We don't celebrate anything special. Another year has passed since the last block party on Berriman Street. Since the last time, Mrs. Kerkashner has passed away. I think it would be appropriate even in the midst of this celebration if we bowed our heads in silence for a few seconds thinking of her in our midst."

He bowed his head and the others did. Mr. and Mrs. Schneider and the Jeffers, the Polinskis, the O'Connors, Mrs. Rizzo, the Estabrooks, the Bernsteins, the Cohens, the Richardsons, even Agnes bowed hers, holding onto Harry's hand, and Miss Horwitz closed her brown oyster eyes; everybody as far as Coin could see had bowed their heads. He couldn't think of Mrs. Kerkashner clearly but he looked at Mr. Kerkashner, standing on the Schneider's stoop alone and bent over with rheumatism, as if he would be able to see her in the weeping man. Bernice, who had been very quiet all evening, was sitting near him with her jumping rope wound around her arm and jacks held loosely in her hand. The moments went by quickly and soon Mr. Foreman was going ahead with the program.

"We're going to have dancing in the streets tonight folks as always, but first Mr. and Mrs. Jeffers have kindly consented to dance one of the whirls they used to do in Trinidad. Mr. and Mrs. Jeffers."

Mrs. Jeffers was spry enough but Mr. Jeffers must have done some fast drinking. Finally he had to stand still in the middle while she whirled around him. Her skirts flew out flat as a plate and the cymbals clashed and clanged out the fast rhythm. Jerome played his harmonica and kept in tune pretty good. Most everyone stamped out the time and even his father patted his feet, not as fast as the rhythm, of course. After they finished and took their bows (Mr. Jeffers nearly fell over) there was laughter from all sides. Mr. Jeffers looked a little bit sick but smiled and smiled at his own mistakes.

Then Leslie O'Connor tried to show off with a tap dance. Everybody laughed and applauded but he wasn't so hot. Coin decided to take up lessons and he'd show them a thing or two. During Mr. Polinski's song, which he sang in Polish, but explained ahead of time that it was about a little boy who was lost in the snow and when he was nearly frozen came upon a wonderful village with golden streets and silver trees and music playing everywhere, Coin looked up the street and saw two figures coming down Esther's side of the block almost at a trot. It was his mother and Mrs. Quick so he let go of Chris's hand and ran toward them, smiling faces changing colors as he passed under the different lights. When he reached them, they were only people from the next block who had sneaked in under the wooden horses that blocked the street off. Mr. Polinski's song that had started so sad with the trumpet wailing low like a baby in a crib was high now. Coin walked back to the musicians' stand kicking a stone ahead of him. If he didn't miss a kick once, his mother would be home soon. Quicker than doodley-squat.

"Doodley-squat."

The dancing began in the streets. The kids danced disjointed and crazy like Pinochio in the story. Coin said to Esther, "I'm Pinochio," and he jerked his head from side to side. Esther said, "Look, Coin, I'm Salome." Look, I'm the king of England, look I'm Rose Marie, look I'm the man in the moon, look Woody's an Indian and Chris' Rudolph Valentino, de da da da de da da dum . . . Agnes was dancing with that old Harry. They danced like the street was oiled, and glide, glide on ice skates. Look at Miss Horwitz staring at them. It was hot and she wore that old fur piece. Woody said it was cat or rabbit fur. De se dum, de. It was made of the three blind mice. They were all panting when the dance was over. Another started up. Harry would walk Agnes home or somewhere and Miss Horwitz would be alone. Ha ha.

Woody suggested that they all go over to the lot and cook up the mickies Mrs. Jeffers had left for them. They screamed past each other. Esther and Abigail and the rest of the girls were last.

"No girls," called Woody and he meant it. "Bernice got jacks and her jumping rope and besides you'll get all dirty."

"How about you?" called Bernice.

"I know how to cook mickies without getting soot anywhere, so put that in your pipe and smoke."

Woody was trying to imitate his father. The girls ran toward Bernice; you could hear them jabbering over the music even. They were choosing sides for the jumping rope.

*My mother and your mother were hanging out the clothes,
My mother gave your mother a punch in the nose.
What color was the blood?*

The answers came in quick succession:
"Blue."
"Red."
"Indigo."
"I-N-D-I-G-O out goes Y-O-U."
"I'm first, I'm first, I'm firs . . ."

Over the fire Woody worked to get all the mickies in the best places for quick baking. And after that there was nothing else to do but wait until they got good and black. Woody watched to see that nobody took one ahead of time. Abie wandered off and Coin squatted by his brother hoping he'd give him a chance to poke the potatoes once in a while. Woody wasn't going to give him a chance. That was that. Coin put his head in his hands and watched the dull coals and heard the faint spit-spitting of the cooking potatoes. One coal was shaped like a butterfly or a red moth and the little flames shooting from it were wings. It lay on top of a potato and the potato was black-eye Susan's center. That's a lot of crap, he thought, using one of Woody's new words. Jerome had his harmonica out and puffed out *There's a Long Long Trail Awinding*.

"Woody," questioned Coin, "do you think it's happened yet?"

"What?"

"Mama."

"Oh, I don't know. Do you think it's gonna happen?"

"Yes," said Coin simply.

"I don't," said Woody and ran to the far side of the fire to see how the other mickies were coming along.

Coin was quiet for a moment. He didn't expect Woody to believe anyhow. He went over by the bandstand.

He liked the sound of the tuba: thump the thump the thump and the way the player had to puff his cheeks out like bubblegum blowing. There was always music spit in the corners of his mouth. The song was long and mournful as a hymn in church. When the band played *O Solo Mio*, Mrs. Renaldo began drinking from her bottle of chianti wine. There was a tear in each eye. He knew he shouldn't stand there like a dummy watching her cry but he didn't know how to leave, especially after she had offered him cakes. During the next song, zippy and longer than *O Solo Mio*, he decided to sit down. The trumpet played the tune high and bright as Chris's sparklers. Mrs. Renaldo reached for Coin and held him closer and closer as the song got higher and thinner. Then she began calling the name. He looked at her slantways. Assunta Assunta Assunta, muttered through the wine-stained tongue, clustered together like red grapes, and deep within him the taste of it grew, grew up to his mouth and he licked his upper lip. Assunta. It was her youngest daughter's name. The one who died on her confirmation day, died all in white, praying on her knees. Candle drip was on her veil, they said. Assunta. It was the trumpet's song.

"Assunta Assunta Assunta o mia Assunta." Finally Mrs. Renaldo opened her eyes, like Esther's sleeping doll. Her mouth and fingers worked the rosary beads which hit against his hands. She pressed him closer and kissed him on the nose. He smelled the wine. Releasing him she stood up, walked so far into the alley he couldn't tell her clothes from the darkness.

He decided the mickies would be ready. On the Richardsons' porch the men played poker in their shirt sleeves. He passed the Carth's. The only one that wasn't decorated with crepe paper. It was dark. He could see Davey at the window peering out. I bet he wished his mother wasn't so mean and he could join the fun. He almost wanted to call to him to come down but he was afraid Davey would say no and besides they weren't going to play with him again anyway. The mickies had been ready. Woody was stuffing himself and he had smudges of soot all over his face and pants. He was grinning with the good taste of what he had baked. The other kids had wandered back too. Abie came running up all out of breath, trying to explain something, and although he was so excited the other kids were too with their mickies.

Woody said, "Calm down, Abie, and have a mickey."
"But she hit me."
"Who?"

"Mrs. Carth."

"Oh, is that all." Woody fished out another mickey.

By the time Coin reached Mrs. Carth's house, she was screaming to the crowd of women lined up at her fence.

"Bad cess to you. Bad cess to all of you. I'll talk what I damn please. Nobody'll tell me what to say. Get the goddamn hell away from here, all you common scum."

The women didn't move. Mrs. Schneider opened the gate and walked to the bottom of the stoop, looked straight up at that old duck Carth.

"You, Mrs. Carth, you better watch how you talk. Poisoning our children and my Abie. I talk, too, Mrs. Carth. I can talk plenty much about much things. About you, Mrs. Carth. You understand what I mean?"

"I bet Mrs. Schneider knows the mystery," Coin thought.

Davey was leaning out of the window on the second story. And as Mrs. Schneider gave her answer to bad cess he let down a shower of confetti like a rainbow snow quivering onto the shoulders of the women, lingering on their hair. They didn't notice. Mrs. Schneider's speech made them think. Mrs. Carth let out a moan like a dog hit by an auto but not killed. Her body sank down by the post. There was blue confetti on her eyelashes. She didn't make another sound. Nobody else did either. The band was playing *Home, Sweet Home*. Davey lit a sparkler and all the women looked up. Mrs. Renaldo was standing near Coin with her eyes shut. She murmured in Italian, turned to go, slipped slightly over a frankfurter roll and then called, in Italian, as she moved away, "Oh, my children, my lost, lost children, be friends before you're dead."

The sparkler startled Mrs. Carth. She snapped her head up toward Davey and yelled like a crazy lunatic.

"You bastard, you bastard, wait till I get you upstairs, I'll kill you."

"It's not his fault, Mrs. Carth. Leave the boy alone."

It was his mother's voice. Coin hadn't seen her at the edge of the crowd. He couldn't see her leg or her arm. Just her face. His heart began to beat fast as the women parted for her to walk up to that duck of a Carth. She didn't move right away. He couldn't bear to look. She was still. She was cured, he knew it. He closed his eyes and said under his breath, "Thank God." It was too bad the block party was over. He wanted to see her dance tonight. Everything was going to be seraphim, though. His mother would be walking so fast he'd have to say come back here, Mama, you're going at breakneck speed. Wait till Popa knew. He'd grin at Agnes and say, I think I'll have half a cup of grape juice.

His mother began to move. Coin's eyes lighted. He wanted Davey to light a million sparklers now. Light up the world, Davey, I'm not mad with you. Mama . . . Mama . . . she dragged her leg. Her arm was hitched up like always. She was going to the gate. Coin couldn't call out or anything. Mama. His neck got tight. Something was around his neck, hanging him. Oh, Mama.

His mother must have forgotten about how he was waiting for her with something tight pressing all around his neck. He swallowed hard and a lump was in his throat and another swallow, the lump was in his stomach, an aching lump was in his stomach, an aching lump. She had forgotten him and was standing in front of Mrs. Carth, that mean old hag, that old dirty duck. His mother was comforting her; she touched the colored papers from her eyelids and said soft things as the other women drifted away and the lights overhead clicked off leaving the magic disappear into only street lamps. Mrs. Quick looked hot and wilted and he didn't want to speak to her. He could go to Woody, but Woody hadn't believed and would say I told you so as quick as a blink; Esther was in bed and she didn't know about it anyway. Popa, Agnes, Bernice. It wasn't any use. His hand went to his pocket to get his handkerchief to wipe his dripping nose and felt the pebble of communion bread from the Sunday long ago. He didn't feel holy any longer. He looked up at the sky as if he could see God and ask about promise. He shot the pebble out from his palm like a marble and it landed in a pile of confetti. There was a blown-up balloon on the picket to Mrs. Schneider's fence. He took it off and wound the string around his finger. He wandered off with the lump aching worse.

As he went past the alley beside Esther's house he heard somebody crying. It sounded like a little echo way in there. Mrs. Renaldo held her body close against the fence with her arms out touching the wood and her long veil fluttering.

"Mrs. Renaldo."

The weeping continued and sniffed off. She turned. He could make out only her face, it was so dark.

"Are you going home, Mrs. Renaldo? I'll take you home." He reached for her hand and the bottle of wine broke against the pavement. He led her out to the sidewalk and down the street to the house. When he closed her door he went to the roof and lay down in the soft tar holding onto the balloon. From the aireyway he still heard a crying. He let the balloon go, watching as it went up several feet and stayed there and then up and up a little more until it got small as a handball and finally lost in all that air. Out of sight and probably lost forever. Did it go high as a star? Did it come down for another little boy? Lost way up there near miracle things that weren't miracle any longer. He wondered about the face of God. He saw the white hair, the beard trailing in the milky way. It was too far to call and too cold up there. All the far away scared him but the warm tar and the warm wind blowing his name up from the aireyway, "Coin, Coin, Coin. Where are you, Coin?" His mother's voice got scattered.

He couldn't sleep down there where he had made all the plans and prayed and they would see him crying and try to comfort him. He felt alone; he was a bird shot in the air and now down in the thick tar he'd have to heal all by himself. They couldn't do a thing. He looked to the balloon for a friend. He searched till the tears blurred and itched his eyes.

"Coin, Coin, Coin."

His name was a gambling game.

"Foreman," Mr. Jeffers said before he was born (Mrs. Quick reported it often with gales of laughing), "Foreman, what did you send for this time, a boy or a girl?"

"A boy. Always a boy."

"Bet it's going to turn out to be a girl."

"No such thing, Jeffers."

"Toss a coin."

Toss a coin for Coin toss a penny toss a dime toss a half dollar toss and toss spin and roll. I want my balloon. Up and up and Coin where are you. I'm going to sleep. Count on the stars . . . God is a liar. And Deaconess Westerfield's hump . . .

He curled up into a ball and began to have a dream.

It was Easter Sunday morning and he was dressed in a sailor suit. White with blue trimmings. He wasn't going with Woody and Bernice to his church. He was going with Chris O'Connor to St. Gabriel's. When they got to the door he could see all the candles and smell the flowers and the big cross with Christ and blood in His hands and His feet and spurting from His side. Coin climbed up the wood to see if the blood was real. It was hard blood. He took out Lon Chaney's dagger and began to stab, stab all over Christ. Nuns became bats with faces made of Argo starch; they flew down the sides. He began to kick. Kicking the pavement and no Chris. The sunlight got in his eyeballs like splinters. Don't rub your eyes, Coin. Don't rub the wood in. He heard singing from a church miles away and ran all the way. Outside they said, "You can't come in."

"My mother's in there."

"You can't come in."

And people were tramping on him. He tried to scratch up the tiles with his fingernails. Then he was free and began to run again like a red devil was chasing him. A truck skidded to a stop and three boys in the back laughed at him. They had on faded blue jeans; there was nothing where the faces were supposed to be. One that was taller than the rest said out of his nothing face, "Little boy, go run and fetch me a tencent bottle of iodine. Don't spill it because I need it."

Coin said, "Oay akay," as he ran off. When he got back with the bottle the truck was starting to move on away.

He yelled, "Here's the iodine!"

"Save it."

"Where'll I find you?"

"We'll be back. We'll be back."

"Coin," his mother's voice said, "I've looked all over for you. I was worried. Don't ever go away like that, we called the police and even Oscar's looking for you."

"Iodine," murmured Coin.

"Come on downstairs and get into bed," his father said.

"Carry him, Popa, he looks worn out."

"All right, Momps."

E̲VER since his mother got sick Coin sneaked a little bit of her medicine each morning. It made him feel better too. There were so many bottles to choose from. The red kind tasted best. Sassparella. The yellow in the big bottle he tasted more than any other, not because he liked it best but there was more of it and he knew it wouldn't be missed. Since the bureau where the medicine was was around the alcove from the bed, his mother never saw. She couldn't move much or speak. Coin always felt big lumps in his throat when she looked at him. He remembered how his mother and Mrs. Renaldo spoke through the eyes.

This morning as he stood by her bed with his shoes shined and his suit all brushed up for the first day of school after Christmas, he wanted to speak and be answered and he felt itchy all over. When she opened her eyes, Coin smiled. Her eyes looked up and down. He was being inspected. He took some lint from off his jacket; her eyes approved. He leaned over and kissed her and ran his pinky through the part in the middle of her hair. It was almost white now. Soft white hair. Thin as dandelions you blow to tell time.

"What's a big boy doing in his mother's lap," Mr. Foreman said wiping snot from his mustache with the big handerchief. Coin scrambled off the bed. "Well, Momps," his father continued, "looks like you'll be up and around before long."

She looked into his eyes. Looked long and the eyelashes blinked. "You're going to be first rate, Momps." He blew loud into the handkerchief. "The Lord's been so good to us he won't stop now. Mr. Courtland gave me dinner money last night. That'll help a good deal. A good deal." He leaned over and kissed her. She closed her eyes. Coin saw him looking into the room from the curtains to the window in the dining room. Mr. Foreman stared for a long time and then left the house.

"Coin, go to school or you'll be late," Agnes said.
"Yes, Agnes."

Mrs. Quick was singing coming up to rub his mother. *"When the roll is called up yonder, I'll be there . . ."*

Agnes rushed to the door. "Please, Mrs. Quick . . ."

"Why, Agnes, excuse me. An old lady forgets sometimes where she is and what's goin' on."

"That's all right. I've just been almost out of my head."

"I know, chile. How's Mrs. Foreman this morning?"

"She took some orange juice."

Mrs. Quick came in breathing hard, her big body fussed with the quiet air as she moved into the room.

Going to school Coin played the Devil's Dishes, stepping on each sidewalk crack to do the devil spite. Miss Horwitz was coming toward him. Old buttermilk Miss Horwitz.

"How's your mother this morning?"

"Drinking orange juice."

"That's fine; nourishment's the best thing. I hope you've been behaving yourself."

"Yes, ma'am."

He missed a crack in the sidewalk and went back to step on it. Fix Miss Buttermilk. He began to whistle between his teeth. It might snow tonight; he and Woody and Chris would build a fort and have a fight. A Christmas tree was burning across the street. The pine smell was sharp. His mother was drinking orange juice. Orange juice and castor oil. They always mixed castor oil with orange juice. He wondered if his mother tasted castor oil. Maybe orange juice would help her talk. He had almost forgotten the sound of her voice. The sky was everywhere white. If somebody pulled a string all the snow would be let loose and come down.

His mother's face hung before him. He began to run. The face ran with him smiling. The hair was made of snow. Snow falling on his mother's face.

He was reading from the geography book before the whole class, with a dunce cap on. Miss Raidin said he had copied some arithmetic from Conrad Fischer. But Conrad was a dumbbell. Anyone would know better than to copy from a dumbbell even if he was your friend.

"No, Miss Raidin, I was just looking at the picture he was drawing."

"Don't be a tattletale. Come up here and read the geography lesson if you're so smart."

"All right," he sulked. He swallowed his piece of chewing gum. It stayed like a bulge in his stomach.

"Where shall I start?"

"At the beginning. Where else would you start?"

Somebody said, "Mr. Smartie." The class giggled. Miss Raidin tapped the desk with her knuckles. I hope she hurt herself, he thought, as he opened the book and began to read:

"1. THE GREAT BALL ON WHICH WE LIVE. The world is our home. It is also the home of many, many other children some of whom live in far-away lands. They are our world brothers and sisters . . .

"Is that enough Miss Raidin?"

"You're so smart. Read on."

"Aw gee." He had left candy on his desk. Conrad might steal it.

> "2. FOOD, SHELTER AND CLOTHING.
> What must any part of the world have in order to be a good home for man? What does every person need in order to live in comfort? . . ." Orange juice and snow. "Let us imagine that we are far out in the fields. The air is bitter cold . . ."

"It's cold in here now, Miss Raidin." That was Crazy Bennie, mad because he was reading without one mistake. After school he'd give him a punch in the nose.

"Continue, Coin."

"How can I read when everybody's talking."

He felt the ruler crack down on his hands. The book fell down and he began to cry. It hadn't hurt. He didn't know why he'd have to begin crying when he was reading better than anybody.

"Go into the wardrobe and slide the door shut. We don't want any crybabies and copy cats in our class. Do we?"

The class chorused NO. In the wardrobe Coin smelled smelly sweaters and old coats. He kneeled down by the wire grate and stuck his tongue out of one of the holes but nobody saw. If he had his candy he could chew up like everything. He closed his eyes and heard his mother talking. She was talking quick, real quick. She was saying dinner money, dinner money, dinner money for the house Coin for the house Coin for a hole as big as a lemon Coin for a lemon as big as

Coin for a hole as big as Coin. When he opened his eyes and peeked out the grate he spied Oscar. Oscar looked ugly as a plop of cigar spit. He didn't want all the kids to see that runt of a big brother. Somebody was pushing the wardrobe door open. His heart began beating fast. What was Oscar doing there?

"Coin," Miss Raidin said, "your brother's waiting to take you home." Her voice was gentle and soft.

He didn't answer a thing as Miss Raidin helped him into his coat. She held him tight and told him to bundle up good. Oscar took his hand. He looked up into the bulging red eyes and felt real sorry for something or other that had nothing to do with Oscar. They walked down the hall, down the steps, into the courtyard before Oscar said, "Mama's very sick."

"Your mother's very sick," Miss Horwitz said. "Don't make any noise."

Coin sat in the hair-cutting chair by the dining room window. Very quiet, very scared. Something was about to happen; when he had come up the street with Oscar, right away he saw the crowd in front of his house. The neighbors. And as he passed through them there were quiet murmurs, "Poor little boy," "Ach, the kint." Even Mrs. Carth was on the edges of the crowd with Davey by her side. She had a handkerchief at her lips. Smelling salts probably. Mrs. Schneider gave Coin a knishe. He could feel it in his pocket now. Far away the bells from St. Gabriel's began ringing. He thought of New Year's Eve when they all stood outside and

Popa made them think they heard the bells of Old Trinity from way across the East River on Wall Street or somewhere.

"Listen to the bells of Old Trinity ringing the New Year in. Don't you hear them, son?"

"A little bit!"

"Better wash the wax out of your ears. You don't want to start the New Year deaf."

But his voice wasn't happy. Mama was lying inside listening to the bells of Old Trinity and she couldn't say nothing, not even Happy New Year, Coin, and Happy New Year, Woody . . .

Through the window between the dining room and the bedroom he could see only parts of everybody; the curtains made them look foggy. They were looking down where the bed was. Mrs. Quick was by the bureau. Her lips moved slowly, and her eyes were looking far off through the walls probably. Miss Horwitz had her arms around Agnes whose teeth bit her lower lip. Bernice and Woody sat together on the low-down bed. The clock ticks kept hitting the silence fast like little musical hammer blows. He gasped frightened as he saw black from the corner of his eyes. Mrs. Renaldo was standing in the doorway to the dining room. She took him in her arms and whispered, whispered, "Holy Mary, Mother of God, Holy Mary, Mother of God," and made the sign of the cross over him. It made him feel better, like when he drank the medicine. She rocked him to and fro in the magenia smell of her bosom. Someone asked, "Where's Coin?" Mrs. Renaldo led him to the bedroom. He tried to pull back.

"See your mother again, mia angel?"

His mother's mouth hadn't moved into a smile for a week but now she smiled pale blue; her lips trembled, kept trembling, trembling and twisted shut. She had smiled at him. The end of a strong breath made her thin hair blow a little. Everything was quiet then. Miss Horwitz opened a window. Silence like nobody was breathing. Only the clock tick talked, "I don't know, ask your mother, I don't know, ask your mother." But all the questions he wanted answered were locked up in the still neck on the bed and the twisted mouth and the closed eyes bulging under the lids.

"Mama?" Coin whispered toward the bed.

"Oh, my God, I can't bear it." Agnes was going to fall.

From across the aireyway came the hitting sound of a stick on a mattress and Abigail Bernstein's voice, "There's one, mother."

"Shut up, can't you; do you want the whole neighborhood should know?"

The covers didn't rise or fall. The clock went just the same. Bernice sat on the low-down bed biting a fingernail, Woody's head was buried on her shoulder and his body shook. Aunt Harriet looked straight at Mama. Mrs. Renaldo made the sign of the cross. Coin never knew when she went out but when he looked for her she was gone. He wanted to follow her some place. Miss Horwitz let out long stinking sighs. Oscar pouted in the corner. His eyes were red like beets. Agnes was stiff as a flagpole. Mrs. Quick looked at her and asked Agnes if she could render up a word of prayer.

"No, Mrs. Quick, no, not now," the words came out squeezed from Agnes' mouth.

"Why chile, prayer is the Christian way. Why if your father were here . . ."

"No praying now!" Agnes' voice scared him.

"Well, I just thought . . ."

"Popa's in Hempstead picking strawberries for Mr. Courtland." Coin thought maybe Agnes was going to laugh. Strawberries and cream.

"Mrs. Quick," Miss Horwitz said, "Agnes knows what to do."

"A word of prayer, a simple pleading word of Christian prayer . . . now you know that would help."

"Get out," Agnes screamed, "get the goddamned hell out of here, you pestering, meddling . . ."

"Oh savior. . . ."

"Please don't pray, please don't. Oh please, please, please." Then Agnes' tears came like a pot boiling over. She went crying toward Mrs. Quick, her hands outstretched like she was blind and needed help. Mrs. Quick's arms folded about her.

"Yes chile, I know. I know. Now don't you know I do. You're the mother now. Cry and cry. Let it all out. Cry Agnes, cry Jesus, you'll feel better."

Then they were all crying except Coin. Hard long doomsday raining.

"Naomi, Naomi, Naomi!" Aunt Harriet's chanting voice tried to open his mother's eyes.

He knew the place. Behind the tall, dead, winter-blown cornstalks, there was the grape arbor Mr. Renaldo had planted in the back yard before he was born. And that's where he went. He sat on a bench. Very still. He saw the white sky through the crossed roots above. A few sparrows hopped and one landed on Coin's knickers . . . the dyed ones. The sun came out like a shining balloon. The sparrow flew toward light. Coin couldn't think of nothing definite. He heard a wailing that seemed to come from Mrs. Renaldo's but he didn't look up. Mrs. Quick had wanted to pray. Well, he'd prayed before and it was no use in the world. For once Agnes was right. Pray to God and write to Santa Claus! God probably spends his time combing the white beard and Santa Claus . . . humph. There was a tin box before him marked Louis Sherry Chocolates that he and Woody had once buried Tobby, their kitten in. It was rusty and scratched. Aunt Harriet's face popped before him. She was repeating over and over what she said when she came early that morning, "I had a feeling something was wrong in Brooklyn, so I put on these clothes and came over to see how Naomi was."

To see how Naomi was. That must be the clock tick now—to see how Naomi was. The sun was in. Snow began coming down. The big, flaky ice cream snow.

"All you do is this," Agnes always said about that kind of snow, "scoop it off the window sill real fast and add vanilla, add sugar and beat very fast . . ."

"Esther, we got ice cream," Coin always said offering Esther a spoonful. "I wish, I wish it snowed every day."

"Thank you, Coin." Esther had good manners.

Snow fell in big clusters making white grapes all over the arbor. If he stayed long enough he'd be a frozen snow man.

Gimmie your aggies Woody for eyes. Aggies for eyes and add vanilla, add sugar, add a paper rose . . .

He saw Undertaker Ward hammer up the gray ribbon crepe; he ran away from the hammering up Berriman Street. Another Coin popped out of him and ran ahead. After a while it came running back into him. But when he spied his father near Pitkin Avenue coming toward him leaning against the twilight-colored snow, one Coin, then two, then three, then a long line of Coins running behind each other toward his father. Their feet hitting the pavement together looked like seven boys tap dancing forward. Then they all folded into him like a pack of cards and he was alone on the white street with his father coming closer with the question on his lips.

"How's your mother?"

The boys flew out of him again and all their seven tongues got stuck tap dancing to the tune of: *How's your mother? how's your mother?* Coin finally said, "Drinking orange juice."

Mr. Foreman nodded and said something but the wind blew his words away.

It snowed until almost midnight on the day his mother died. Of all the snowstorms he could remember, Coin knew this was the one he would remember until the rest of his life. This was the day his mother . . . he wouldn't form the words *died* or *dead* with his lips or the other ways they talked: *she passed away, she's gone, she's in the arms of Jesus, your mother has passed.* Passed. Passed to where? Heaven? Up there the night was white. He had been in the room and nothing went out of the room. *Her spirit has gone to God.* He had seen nothing. When he saw the little man, there was sunlight at least and curtains and a reason for seeing. They said his mother was in the front room. *She's resting at last. Eternal peace.* The word "nigger" nagged in his mind. He hadn't understood then either. He would never understand anything. Everyone knew but him. *She's resting on the bosom of Jesus.* Woody said only women had bosoms. Jesus was a man with a long skirt and holding a lamb to his bosom. He didn't care who He was. God, Jesus, The Holy Ghost, eternal spirits and the street turned all today into a white snow miracle. No cars could get by until morning. No snow forts forever. There were hardly any footsteps in the snow. All the shades were pulled inside. The streetlamps stamped the snow with diamond circles.

He lay on the bed that night wondering and trying to sleep, when the bell rang sharp. He heard Agnes tiptoeing to the dining room door and Miss Horwitz ask somebody how they got here in the snow and all.

"Have you ten cents in your purse?" Agnes asked Miss Horwitz.

"Ten cents is too big a tip, Agnes. You'll need your change."

"Fartsafongoo," whispered Coin to himself. "Fartsafongoo all over Miss Horwitz."

"It's a letter from my uncle."

"Pity he couldn't write after you told him your mother was sick and send some money."

Coin heard the tearing of the envelope and Agnes talking, "Listen to this Lucy . . . it's for Mama . . . for Mama . . ." Coin was listening aloud.

"My dear Sister Naomi, It has been some time since I have had a letter in your hand . . ."

Before he was born his mother could write in her hand. ". . . I got a letter from niece Agnes saying that you were very sick and I hear from Sister Harriet occasionally, I understand that she is not quite so well but able to work. I sent her a herb almanac and she wrote out some recipes and said that she was going to give them to you. You have been ailing a long time. I am giving some advice from my own personal and I think it would be wise to try it anyway . . ."

"Don't read any more, Agnes," Miss Horwitz said softly, but Agnes continued like she couldn't stop.

". . . The doctors today are nothing but professional quacks and smart ellicks. . . ."

Bernice said Woody was a smart ellick. Woody's no doctor. Fartsafongoo.

". . . They just try to give you enough medicine to ease the pain but it won't built you up or Eliminate the poisons that are in the system. From your case you have not enough iron in the blood . . ."

"Agnes!" Miss Horwitz talked higher. Agnes kept on. ". . . this formula that I recommend I think will help you and do you a great deal of good and I think you should try it, it won't hurt you it is an old-fashioned Herb tonic I make myself and I gave Harriet some of it when she was tired and she likes it very much its not so costly and much better than the Doctors medicine because most of the medicine the Doctors use is ignorance and inorganic and it is too hard on the heart and do you more harm than good but this will not hurt your heart . . ."

"It won't hurt her heart now. Nothing will, nothing ever again, Lucy."

Agnes' voice got higher and some crying was in it. ". . . but will clean the entire system from your head to your foot. you can take the Doctors medicine too if you want to but it won't make any difference. This medicine will be like Moses Rod which swallowed up all the others . . ."

Coin wondered what it tasted like, what color it was and how it smelled. He decided it must be strong enough to make you swallow up all the others. A tune began in his head, *"There's a soldier in the grass with a bullet up his ass."*

Then Agnes' voice drowned it out. He was glad. ". . . you should not eat too many sweets and too sticky food or beef and pork. but eat liver and eggs. chicken, veal, Bacon. Fish all poultry. Carrots, beets and Spinach. . . ."

Eat magenia, eat Mrs. Renaldo's magenia smell, eat lima bean stew. He turned restlessly on the bed and hung his head over the side staring at the empty bed.

His father wasn't home. He was out trying to get some money from Mr. Courtland. Before he went out Agnes had said, "But the insurance money, Popa, is enough."

"There is no insurance, daught."

"But there is . . ."

"It lapsed. I let it lapse. There wasn't money and then I forgot . . . I just forgot."

He was glad Agnes didn't say anything to his father. His face was gray as the crepe on the front door as he went out of the house and Coin watched his dark body plowing through the snow to a telephone to ask Mr. Courtland for . . . for strawberries and cream from Hempstead. Coin's head jerked back onto the pillow and Agnes' voice droned on and on, the words running into each other and crying into his ears. He felt sorry for Agnes because she couldn't stop reading.

". . . Here is the formula and I am sending you some circulars read them carefully. and follow the directions. You order them and try them and if they don't work I will reimburse you for every dollar that you spend so you won't lose anything. I recommend formula. 120 Virginia Snake Root compound which will be $1.50 and other additional roots. wich will be 25¢ for each Root. the following Mullein Skunk cabbage, Pork root, Golden seal, Solomon Seal, Bayberry Bark. which will be $3.00 plus 15¢ for postage. Take a cup full of these herbs and Put 2 quarts of water and boil for $2\frac{1}{2}$ hours slowly. then strain into a pitcher but dont dump it boiled your herbs 4 times and mix all your medicine to gether and put into quart jars and set in your cupboard dont use any tin or allumen to cook them in use Porcelain Utensils I send love to all your brother Cousin Troy Starr.

"The blind fool," Miss Horwi . . . He was almost asleep again and for a moment he thought he saw some snakes in mason fruit jars swimming around laughing and singing: "I send love your Troy Starr and Solomon Bayberry drink this and see Moses Rod. . . ." There was a scream and he sat up in bed like he'd been slapped. Pretty soon Aunt Harriet hurried through the room and the voices mounted into a scramble . . . for Bayberry bark. . . .

Because Aunt Harriet was the only one who had ever seen Uncle Troy Starr, she had to go to the station to meet him. The telegram had said, "ARRIVING PENNSYLVANIA STATION 6:35." Coin begged to go because the house was so crowded now with the old sisters from the church and it was too cold to wander around outside. Everyone patted him too much and said wasn't it a shame that he was without a mother. But in a way it was something like Christmas. There was snow and all kinds of food and candy. He had a new suit marred by an armband to show that his mother was dead. He asked Miss Horwitz when she was sewing it on did he really have to wear that on his new suit. She told him to shut up and go on about his business. He didn't have any business. Sometimes too in all the hustle and bustle he almost forgot what had happened. But when he sat very still and closed his eyes he knew his mother was there and in his mind he listened to her talk and went over the times they had after school together. Like shopping on Blake Avenue, when they saw the 10 Commandments together at the Montaulk Theatre: Breaking the Golden Calf. The kids on the block treated him special too. They didn't speak loud when he was around. If he talked they listened as if everything he said had an aggie in it for them. Esther trailed him when he was outside. Her little red freckled face didn't smile. She asked everytime she saw him, "My mother wants to know if she can do anything for you."

"I'm okay, Esther."

"Can I help you, Coin?" And he wanted to dart away to the grape arbor. But when they had caught him out there after his mother died, Agnes asked him if he wanted to catch his death of pneumonia. Didn't she have enough trouble.

"If I catch you sitting in the cold again, I'll forget myself and give you a slap you won't forget."

"Yes, Agnes." He looked up at her. Mrs. Quick had declared that Agnes was his mother now. He didn't believe it. His mother was his mother. Not Agnes, not nobody.

"Yes, Agnes."

"I won't slap you, I didn't mean that, I'm just tired, Coin, that's all."

Aunt Harriet and Coin stood at the top of a flight of stairs waiting for the train people to come up. Aunt Harriet's black veil thrown over her made her face look like it was coming out of a black tunnel. He loved Aunt Harriet. She wasn't bossy like Miss Horwitz and she always brought peanuts to the house when she came except this last time. And she never was late anywhere. If she took Woody and Coin to the circus she came hours early and they always got the best seats way up so they could look down and see everything at once.

"Aunt Harriet will never be late to her own funeral," Mrs. Foreman said as a joke once.

"I declare, Harriet, the way you get to a station hours ahead and sit there eating peanuts and frankfurters gives me a chill. I can always tell how long you've been waiting by the pile of peanut shells. How can you wait that long?"

"Better late than never," Aunt Harriet laughed in answer.

That's why she's standing first one foot and then another now, Coin thought, the train's late.

"If a train comes in late they ought to give you half your money back. Suppose you had a business engagement or something."

Her hand rested on his head and drummed a tune. Probably a hymn. She drummed slow and steady.

"Here they come." The hymn on his head stopped. A few people came up slowly with tired steps, dragging all kinds of bags by their sides, newspaper bundles too. They kept coming up like all those clowns out of the one auto at the circus. The whole world might be down coming up.

"I do hope he's on this train." The people kept dragging up until they sprinkled out to a few and then no one at all, except a conductor scratching an island of hair on his bald head. Baldy bean.

> *Wash them dishes,*
> *Wash them clean*
> *As Mr. Hendrick's*
> *Baldy bean.*

"What did you say, Coin?"

"Nothing."

The greeting crowd began to go away. Just as Aunt Harriet was turning to go they spied him coming slowly up the stairs, knocking with a stick to see by.

"Stay here, Coin," and Aunt Harriet flew down the stairs to help him up. They stopped on a landing and kissed. He kept feeling her face. Coming up Uncle Troy Starr looked like he had stepped out of one of those funny mirrors with a caved-in belly at Luna Park. Coin giggled in his throat remembering how he had looked a mile fat in one and skinny as a thermometer in another. At the top Aunt Harriet said, "Troy, this is Naomi's baby, Coin."

Uncle Troy's hand reached out for his face and touched it all over. It tickled. His voice was fat and juicy as Woody's singing and he was the color of grapefruit.

"Why look at this man here. And good-looking, too. You mean to tell me, Sister Harriet," and he looked in the opposite direction from his sister, "that somebody as handsome as this boy is kin to me."

He laughed, opening his mouth wide showing some

gold teeth and a lot of pink gum, laughed so that Coin liked him. He shook Coin. "Well, son, say something to your uncle, it sure is good to see you."

See! His hand was still on Coin's face. It smelled like bread just out of the oven.

"Hello, Uncle Troy."

"Is that all you've got to say?"

"Yes, sir." The big laugh came again.

"Well, come on here, Harriet, let's get on."

"Where's your bags?"

"Had 'em sent on."

"Coin, take Uncle Troy's hand." The grip was strong as a vise.

"Harriet, I reckon we ought to take a taxicab."

"Good gracious, that's a fortune."

"I'm kinda tired. I reckon I can afford a taxicab. Just came back from one of my trips."

Coin looked at him again from head to foot. He could stare because he wouldn't be seen. A dark-blue Sunday suit and a black hat. He was dressed up almost as good as Deacon Ferebee.

As soon as the taxicab stopped, Coin noticed the crepe. A shadow sliced it in half. The white flowers seemed made out of snow and some others looked like the red peppers Mrs. Renaldo cooked with. An unseen hand of wind shivered through the flowers as if it were too nervous to choke them. A long green tail swayed back and forth. This was the new sign by the door of his house and he hated it.

HE WOKE up before anybody else on the day of his mother's funeral. Leaning out of the low-down bed, he looked way into the front room where his father slept in his stocking feet, his mouth snoring toward the casket. Gas jet light surrounded his head. He had stayed there all last night and the night before.

Uncle Troy was sleeping in his father's place across the way. Coin tiptoed into the bathroom. On the medicine chest his uncle's teeth, with pieces of last night's dinner, seemed alive as if they had just taken a bite out of something good and held it tight for keeps. Coming back to the low-down bed he stopped to stare at his uncle's uncovered body. He tried to fit the teeth into the squeezed-in sucking jaws. Around the neck was wrinkled. Fat folds of stomach folded over his belly button like lips. Spindly legs were crossed, covering his business. That was what old looked like under the clothes. He and Woody had discussed it often.

"Whatcha bet they're wrinkled underneath like the face and hands?"

Coin didn't answer his brother because he didn't know, so couldn't bet. All the grapefruit-colored flesh there in the bed had always seemed wrinkled that way. He turned to Woody who had awakened, "Woody, whatcha gonna do with the quarters Uncle Troy gave you?"

"Buy some flowers, I suppose."

Everyone was giving flowers. He knew Woody didn't want to be left out. Crepes with flowers and weeping under black veils. Death! They were all like Mrs. Renaldo now: looking in on the dead for a final howdy-do visit. He thought of funerals on Berriman Street.

The Jews didn't wear veils or black or buy flowers or look at the dead. They kept house-clothes on and they buried before sundown. "Quick, before they rot," Woody said. They cried, though, almost as much as at Italian funerals where bands played *Nearer My God to Thee* and coaches and coaches of flowers and all the bowing before the cross and the priest swinging incense that smelled into the street. Italians screamed all night. They looked in the casket all right and some fell out crying and peering. Coin decided he wouldn't look into the casket no matter how many times the old sisters asked. He knew his mother was in the gray plush box lined with wrinkled white like whipped cream. She was in there. She was not! He wouldn't never, never, never, never, look. That was that.

"Woody, did you look in?"

"Yeah."

Coin gave Woody all his quarters. Woody snatched them greedily.

For two days now Coin had hated flowers. He had one particular white carnation picked out to tear off the crepe and stamp in the snow. And when he did that there was a red pepper rose he was going to stamp on top of it. That would be some revenge. So many flowers in the wintertime for a celebration it seemed. There were flowers at weddings, and at graduations the girls received a bouquet, and at confirmations in the Catholic churches. In the spring the lots were filled with daisies and wild roses, (dandelions didn't count), violets, apple trees blooming and bitter black cherry trees. Flowers at funerals didn't fit at all unless they buried the dead to grow, buried cats and dogs, buried treasures to spend. He tore the glove off his left hand, bit quickly at his pinky, sawed the nail between his teeth with his tongue. He didn't want to go into the house although there was nothing to do at the door.

The house seemed so small with the church sisters,

neighbors and relatives crowding over each inch. The back of the house smelled close of a trillion dishes cooking. The rest of the house had the damp in-the-woods flower odor. A little blood trickled from his pinky. He sucked it up. The fire was out in the front room where the casket was. They said to keep the body fresh. Of course, the old sisters never uttered the name. It was always the body, or her or our sister. The gaslights shone dim in that room spreading a haunted-house look in the air. And they were dressed up too, everybody. Esther said that when a Jew dies the family sat in sackcloth and ashes and "sitinshiver." This was different, this seemed a celebration because his mother was not there. Someway the hustle and bustle and the new clothes and all made him mad and angry. Even the new blue serge he had on with the black band he got only because his mother was dead. He had wanted a new suit for a long time instead of the hand-me-downs from Mr. Courtland's boys.

He sat on a box from Mr. Altar's grocery store to watch and wait. They said the funeral was set for one o'clock. It was only eleven.

Esther came over. They watched a bird fly from Abie's roof to a telephone wire.

"I bet he gets a shock."

"Birds are *it*, Coin, not he or she, and they have something in their feet that protects them," Esther said softly.

Little clouds of their breath came full and trailed away in unison. They waited for the bird to fly away, but more birds joined. The telephone wire shivered as their songs began in sharp duck screeches.

"Starlings. They're not afraid of anything. Not even winter."

"I didn't know that," Coin sighed. His pinky hurt.

"Coin . . . ?" Esther's voice came from far away. He was looking at the crepe again. He felt cold revenge-flowers in his hand almost.

"Coin . . . my . . . my mother's going to the funeral. I'm going too." She ran back to her porch, watching Coin from a distance. Coin felt her eyes.

A florist car scrubbed up the street with the chains making snow scoot. The birds flew away together. Coin stood in front of the crepe.

"Hey, kid," the driver called, "this 309 Berriman Street?"

"No," answered Coin; he heard his voice flat and definite, "that's down the street."

The truck moved off slowly. Halfway down the street it backed back.

The driver got out with a big round wreath. Planted in the middle of the flowers was a purple clock, made of cardboard, with white hands set to the time his mother died.

"You don't know your ass from your elbow," the driver told Coin.

Reverend Brooks came down the street in his black minister's clothes and stopped to pat Coin's head before he followed the big wreath into the vestibule. Coin knew he had come to discuss the final plans for the funeral. Popa and Agnes had had an argument over it last night after he had gone to bed. He heard them all right and seen them too because he slept on the outside and could look into the front room. Woody and Uncle Troy had been snoring. Woody's snore was a little bit behind. Agnes had just tried on her veil and her face seemed far away. As she talked her breath moved the thin black in and out.

"Popa," Agnes had said, "please, no big funeral. Make it simple and quiet with only the family."

"No, daught, your mother stood for something in the church and community. It wouldn't be fair to keep those who loved her from honoring her."

"Those who loved her," Agnes' voice had a sneer in it, "those old hypocrites who wouldn't give you a slice of bread without advertising it over the neighborhood. She wasn't their mother. Mama was quiet with no fuss and you want to make a show. . . ."

"It's only right that . . ."

"Only right for what, Popa. For you, for Reverend Brooks, for the whole bunch that live and breathe death and wakes and funerals. For God's sake, Popa . . . stop all that, I won't be able to stand it. And the children. Are you going to make them go through all that. Christ!"

"I've told you and I've told you to stop taking the Lord's name in vain."

"They're taking Mama in vain. Remember Mr. Zeno's funeral. That was going to be nice and quiet, too."

"Nothing like that."

"How do you know? Once they get started they get carried away."

"They'll follow my wishes," Popa said and took out one of his dinner handkerchiefs to blow his nose.

"Your wishes. Popa, you'll never learn. Just like you kept on having children, children, children and poor as a church mouse. When Mama told me Coin was coming, I was disgusted. Nine children, half of them dead and you kept right on. Twenty-five dollars a week and you bred like you earned a million . . ."

"Daught, please."

". . . a million fine ideas. And now I'll have to take over. Waste my life on a bunch of snotty nose brats. . . ."

Mr. Foreman raised his hand and smacked her hard as he had smacked Oscar.

"You shut up talking to your father this way. What would she think?"

It was good for Agnes but Coin cried with her. His tears tasted bitter. They had not wanted him to be delivered at all. Not special, not anyway.

Popa stood there like he was going to fall, then went over to the gray casket, slid his hand over the plate where the name was carved.

Silence except for the snores. Silence except for the ticking clock.

Low, very low, Popa spoke, "Leave me alone, daught, here for a minute. There are things you don't understand. The Lord tells so little, when you are young. He tells . . . You may be right. I . . . I couldn't make enough but I tried to be a good father and I love my children and I loved their mother. Leave me with her."

"Yes, Popa, yes." Agnes had come through the room holding the hat and the veil. He felt her pause by the cot, lean down to straighten the covers and stroke his head. When her fingers felt his tears, he heard her cry again. She went into the bathroom. The water ran and ran.

He turned to see if Esther was still watching. She had gone inside. He hesitated about taking the two flowers from the crepe for stamping and deciding not to, went into the vestibule and followed Reverend Brooks up the steps. The dining room was filled as usual with people sitting around holding their hands in their laps or whispering to the one beside them. In the kitchen Deaconess Redmond leaned over the stove. As he passed all of them they just shook their heads, sorry for him, or reached to hug. He snatched out of their arms.

"The poor child's taken with grief. Remember the night of his baptism."

"It was beautiful. Well, at least he's a Christian and the Lord's the best comfort. . . ."

He headed directly for the bathroom. Inside he decided to brush his teeth. He brushed until his mouth was sore. He did number one and flushed the toilet watching the swirl of water spin down and the bowl fill up again. He couldn't think of nothing else to do so he unhitched the latch. As he opened the door he saw Deaconess Redmond in the kitchen alone, sticking his mother's best spoons . . . the company silver she had gotten as a wedding present from Mrs. Tyler . . . into her bosom. He eased the door to a crack and just watched her. The wart flared out and she panted. The last spoon jutted out a little and she was ramming it in. He sneezed as loud as he could and opened the door to full and looked her in the eye. The spoon still stuck out. At last I know who stole the collection plate money Mrs. Quick talked about, Coin thought.

"Bless the Lord, honey," she giggled twitching, putting a dish towel over her bosom and wiping, "I was trying to get this stain off my dress where I done spilled some grease cooking your dinner for later on." Her voice hit your, trailed off into another giggle. "Why, Coin, did you see my pocketbook. I laid it around here somewhere." Turning like she was looking, he watched her grab the poking-out spoon and lay it on the sink. She left the others in. "I had something in that pocketbook for you."

Coin wanted to spit in her wart. Instead he answered, "I don't want nothing from you, Deaconess Redmond."

He went over to the sink, picked up the spoon, put it in the drawer, and started into the bedroom with her voice calling after him in gravy whispers.

Those who were going in the swanky cars were lined against the walls of the apartment from the front room back to the dining room. Six deacons dressed in dark suits filed in and Undertaker Ward handed each of them white gloves. The flowers had been removed earlier by the undertaker's men but the smell remained. The deacons took their places on either side of the casket and lifted it by the handles. As they moved toward the door Mr. Foreman turned his head the other way. Coin remembered Popa never wanted to see one of his own carried out. He looked almost gray in the face and his mouth trembled. Agnes stood on one side of him. Beside her Mrs. Quick, in her nurse's outfit, fidgeted. Her bag was handy. She peered into veiled and unveiled faces for signs of needing spirits of ammonia or smelling salts. Coin *knew* she was waiting. At every funeral she waited, many times she was needed too.

Coin, Woody and Bernice stood at the head of the steps looking down past the black heads to the vestibule where the deacons had lifted the casket to their shoulders. They carried their burden steady out the front door. Undertaker Ward appeared below with a list in his hand and began calling names like tickets to admission.

"Deacon O. E. Foreman and daughter." Popa and Agnes walked out of sight. Those on the steps moved down one. Mrs. Quick waited on the sidelines with her bag looking into faces as they passed her by, patting each one for comfort. Deaconess Redmond was near her.

"Mr. Troy Starr and Mrs. Harriet Butler." They walked out of sight. Everyone moved down one.

"Master Woodrow Foreman, Miss Bernice Foreman, Master Coin Foreman." Undertaker Ward pointed to the long black Cadillac at the curb. Woody marched ahead with Bernice because Coin was stopped by Deaconess Redmond who thrust something under his arm and gave him her heavy pat. He paused at the doorway. Abie's face was real sad standing by his mother. His nose was running as usual. Esther was at the church already, he supposed. Chris O'Conner dangled a baseball mitt, in winter too, in his left hand. Coin slipped on the ice going to the car and landed on his behind. The driver helped him up. As he got in, Woody and Bernice were giggling.

In the car he turned away from them and saw Mrs. Carth crying at the edge of the crowd. His behind stung. Master Coin Foreman, Master Coin Foreman. The street was icy white, the porches crowded in all directions. They were crying real tears, their mouths worked goodbyes. They wept Mrs. Renaldo tears, black veils weeping.

Where was Mrs. Renaldo? Mrs. Quick said she was upstairs in her apartment holding her rosary beads, mumbling heathen prayers for his mother . . . she said, let her have her rusty beads, poor soul, she's lived with the dead too long. Master Coin Foreman may take a step to the right, to the left, right. Undertaker Ward folded the list before he took the crepe off the door. The red pepper flowers were withered frozen. The white carnations were frozen brown. The last one out of the house was Miss Horwitz. She headed straight for their Cadillac. Woody said a dirty word. Bernice began to pout.

At the church the procession went up the stairs instead of down like at the house. Coin wondered what took the line so long to get into the church. He leaned first on one foot, then on the other. Thank goodness, Miss Horwitz has gone somewhere. To Agnes probably.

On the way to church she had deviled them all. She blessed Woody out because he had some aggies. When Woody explained that he always carried his best aggies no matter where he was going, she told him he was mean and insensitive. Because Bernice's hair shot from under her hat, she called her a sloppy black child who would never amount to anything. No sooner had Coin gotten in the car before she told him he was dirty-minded because he was stroking his behind. He told her that it hurt from the fall. She replied that it would hurt more by the time Agnes taught him not to be so clumsy. And so on forever. But Coin didn't mind too much. He knew she was nervous and had helped his mother many times. She kept bubbling her lips and clapping her purse open and closed.

As they neared the entrance to upstairs he heard the music of *Asa's Death*. Miss Van Epps played that often for them in music hour. The class would sing the first two bars to the words, "Asa's Death from Peer Gynt by Edward Griegeeg." Now it sounded different. All things left him and the music swelling in long sad notes covered everything. The familiar funeral words Reverend Brooks spoke as he headed the procession were clear to him for the first time. They meant all funerals, all dead. They were heavy stones of sorrow Reverend

Brooks rolled down the aisle toward the organ, toward the deaconesses ranged around the rostrum with the flowers, waiting to receive the casket.

"I am the resurrection and the life and the light, he that believeth in me though he were dead yet shall he live. Man that is born of woman hath but a short time to live and his life is filled with sorrow . . ."

Reverend Brooks mounted the pulpit. The family and relatives sat in the front rows. Coin was behind his father. The deacons set the casket on stands. Undertaker Ward and his helpers took the wreaths from the deaconesses one by one and arranged them around the casket. The wreath that Agnes and Popa sent was laid on top. The congregation, that had been standing as the coffin rode down the aisles on the shoulders of the deacons, sat at a nod from Reverend Brooks.

"Let us pray," he said. Heads bowed together.

"Dear heavenly father, we come before Thee to pay our last respects to one of Thy faithful servants who has labored long in Thy vineyard and passed from out our midst to Thy throne. We cannot offer up prayers of grief for one who so richly deserves her reward. We only ask comfort in this hour for her spouse and her children who are not yet prepared to set out without the guiding hand of a mother. Bless them, comfort them, let Thy light shine upon them.

"We know that Thou canst open doors and nobody can close them, that Thou canst close doors and no man can open them. We do not ask Thy explanation, we only ask Thy guidance.

"We know that words are things, that they have the power to raise us up or bow us down. We pray that the words in this hour will raise us up until we understand, somewhat, Thy will. Amen.

"The congregation will now sing the first and last verses of Abide With Me. Page one hundred forty-four in the hymnal."

The organ started in a whisper. The congregation arose and sang the verses low, not to disturb the dead.

The darkness deepens Lord with me abide . . .

The sun broke through the stained-glass window, like it had on the day he had become a Christian, and sprayed long fingers of light. Once his mother had sung that song while she was cooking. He could see her now stirring the food with her good hand. Stirring the tune into the pot. Stirring slow. Stirring abide with me.

*When others helpless fail and comforts flee,
In life, in death, oh Lord, abide with me.*

Out of the corner of his eye Coin saw Mrs. Quick go hopping to Aunt Harriet. The veil was lifted up and a bottle of smelling salts thrust under. A few of the deaconesses nearby could hardly sing for looking.

In life, in death, oh Lord, abide with me.

Deacon Loring, who had arisen with difficulty from his chair, was going to read the obituary from the family. Popa had worked hard on it two nights ago, writing and crossing out, reading aloud to Agnes, making corrections.

The bass drum in Deacon Loring's voice began to sound. Woody nudged Coin for some special reason he didn't understand, probably the same old joke about the Deacon's fat. Coin didn't nudge back.

"Brooklyn, New York, February nineteenth, nineteen twenty-six. Mrs. Naomi Starr Foreman was born in Boydon, Virginia, fifty-four years ago, the daughter of Clara and Raymond Starr. She spent the early years of her life in that community and at the age of seventeen went to Hartsorn Seminary for girls in Richmond, where she studied to be a teacher. After graduating from that institution with high honors, she returned to Boydon to teach in the elementary schools. In eighteen hundred and ninety-eight she met and married Oscar Emerson Foreman, a young newspaper man. The Lord blessed that union with nine children. . . ."

Agnes was looking at Popa. Popa stared straight ahead. Coin remembered last night and how Agnes felt. The whole church seemed empty except for him and the image of his mother dragging her foot down Blake Avenue with a banana in her hand for him. He hugged his arms in, closed his eyes.

". . . The Foremans moved to Brooklyn, New York, July nineteen hundred and immediately joined the Corinthian Baptist Church where they have been members ever since. She served the church in various capacities. She was, at the time of her death, vice-president of the Brooklyn Mother's Club, which she was instrumental in founding, a member of the Dorcas Society, the Willing Workers' Club, a Daughter of the Eastern

Star, a member of the Pastor's Aid Society and the Deaconess Board number one. . . ."

Coin saw Deaconess Redmond take out her handkerchief. She's a crook and a hypocrite and here she is carrying on to make a lie. He remembered, too, how she had shot questions at him after he was converted. It all mixed him up. That white dress and holy, holy on the lips. And she's a crook. He didn't have any plans yet but when he got home he'd see if all the spoons were there. If not he'd sic Miss Horwitz on her. That would make her holler.

". . . nine years ago after the birth of her last child she suffered a stroke. . . ."

He was on trial; he was accused. He felt alone. The church was empty. He was condemned to take communion forever.

". . . on Christmas night of last year she suffered a second stroke from which she never recovered. She was a servant of God who never failed her duties. . . ."

Deaconess Redmond uttered a loud amen and amens followed from the deaconesses' corner in ragged order. Agnes gave Popa a hard stare.

". . . a beloved wife and a sainted mother. We shall miss her deep and hard, forever, as long as we live. There is an empty place at our table. If she were alive now she would say, 'I have lived my life, I have kept the faith and now I am ready to be rendered up.' "

Coin heard her say those words once bending over the washtub, scrubbing winter longies with one hand, he could just hear her saying them.

"She leaves to mourn her loss, a husband, Oscar Emerson Foreman, and five children: Agnes, Oscar, Jr., Bernice, Woodrow and Coin, one sister, Harriet Starr Butler, a brother, Troy Starr and a host of friends and relatives. Signed, The Family."

There was a stir in the church as the names of the motherless were called off. Coin felt eyes on him from every direction and he took Woody's hand. It was thrust away. At that moment the tune of, *Yes, We Have No Bananas, We Have No Bananas Today,* started in his head.

Aunt Harriet rose and went to the deaconesses' room. Mrs. Quick rushed after her and closed the door carefully as if the service would interfere with her administrations. Coin heard Deaconess Redmond whisper to Deaconess Westerfield, "Guess she can't bear it, poor soul."

Deaconess Westerfield hunched her shoulders in sympathy, it looked like. The lump on her back seemed another shoulder going perpendicular.

"Those who have condolences, kindly move forward," Deacon Loring said. There was rustling, paper rattling. From all directions men in black and women in white hoover aprons seemed to trot forward panting a little. They reminded Coin of black and white birds heading for a pile of crumbs. One by one they fled into position beside the black hill, Deacon Loring, and read words of comfort from Virginia, New York, Staten Island, New Jersey, from societies and clubs, from organizations his father was a member of, from Agnes' school. They read out loud and full as if they were to be marked.

"Jersey City, New Jersey. Whereas it has pleased Almighty God in his Divine wisdom to remove from out our midst the late Naomi Starr Foreman, our fellow worker . . ."

Yes, we have no bananas, we have no bananas today,
We got old-fashioned tomatoes, Long Island potatoes,
But, yes, we have no bananas, we have no bananas today . . .

The tune zizzed around in his head slowly, slowly, faint and sharp. He shook his head a little to get it out. Mrs. Quick was watching him. Her bosom swelled with a desire to use smelling salts on him, he knew. She wanted him for a victim now that she had brought Aunt Harriet back shaking and stumbling.

". . . and whereas her manifest interests in movements affecting the welfare and progress of all the people was indicated in her connections with the social, benevolent and family institutions . . ."

We got string beans and scallions,
Corn and rapscallions,
We have no bananas today, we have no bananas to . . .

Coin flexed the muscles in his forehead to see if that did any good. Then he tried to concentrate on nothing at all and the tune faded. The best thing to do was sit like a mummy.

"Therefore be it resolved that the officers and members of the Brooklyn Mother's Club . . ."

Professor Myers was warming the organ up. The resolves and whereases would end soon.

". . . be it further resolved that a copy of these resolutions be sent to the bereaved family and that a copy be spread upon the minutes of this organization. Signed: The Brooklyn Mother's Club. Addie Kate Freneau, President, Mammie Simpson, Secretary, Louise Sawyer, Recording Secretary."

Deacon Loring waved the readers away. The organ started. Sister Sarah Russell, in the choir loft, rose, adjusting her book before her, opened her mouth.

Yes, we have no bananas, we have no bananas. . . .

He knew he was going crazy. The organ took up the tune. The whole church heard the song that was running faster and faster in his head.

"I love this fleet as a bird song," Deaconess Redmond whispered to her neighbor. "They played it at Sister Sylvia Harris' rites and you should have heard the . . ."

The two songs were racing in his head; they tangled with each other. He didn't care where he was or what was happening; he had to get out.

Fleet as a bird that flies to rest,
Yes, we have no bananas, we have no bananas today . . .
Fleet as a bird to the mountains,
We got all kinds of onions
Carrots and bunions but
Fleet as a bird to the heavens . . .

With terrible effort, the sweat pouring off him in the cold church, he got up. Mrs. Quick rushed over with her bag and her bosom. He knew that he had made a mistake. They would all be saying that he was beside himself with grief. He was beside himself all right.

"Sh, sh, honey. I got something here to make you feel better. I have it right here. Now, you know I have," she whispered.

In the deacons' room, Mrs. Quick made him sit down. She wiped his face with alcohol and thrust the smelling salts into his nose telling him to breathe deep, oh, breathe deep. She seemed delighted with herself. She kissed him on the cheek, she held his head against her bosom, she hummed. She reached into her bag for ginger snaps and put them in his mouth. She opened a window. The air brushed the songs away although the room trembled with the vibrations of the organ. He sat by the window.

"That's right, you just sit there for a while. I'll be back. There may be others in distress."

On the floor was the package Deaconess Redmond had given him. He had brought it with him. Inside was a large slice of sweet potato pie (his favorite) and two fifty-cent pieces. He threw the box out of the window. The money went plunk outside. Once over a year ago his mother had asked him to peel some potatoes while she prepared crust. He was in such a hurry to go out, he peeled fast and furious, leaving big pieces of good potato on skins he threw rapidly into the garbage can. After a while his mother came in for the potatoes. She just looked at the puny ugly-shaped hunks Coin had dropped into the colander. Her eyes had filled with tears. "Coin, Coin, look at all this waste. You could do better than this. We're poor. You've always had enough to eat; your father sees to that but we can't waste anything. Do you hear, not even a pinch of salt. Now I want you to remember that when you sit down to dinner. There won't be any pie for you. You've peeled your share away."

That was the first and last time his mother had ever really scolded him. He couldn't look her in the eye. All he had said was, "Abie's waiting for me." He hung his head, slipped out the door. He didn't enjoy the games that afternoon. He didn't win; he didn't deserve to.

The door was opening. Mrs. Quick had come to take him back. She held his hand and when he tried to pull away she took a harder grip.

When he was seated, his father turned and asked, "You all right, son?"

"I'm okay, Popa."

Reverend Brooks was just announcing the text.

"Proverbs 31:10. 'Who can find a virtuous woman? for her price *is* far above rubies!' I read again: 'Who can find a virtuous woman? for her price *is* far above rubies.' And further: 'Her children arise up, and call her blessed; her husband also, and he praiseth her.'

"In this hour that seems so dark to us. This death hour when our eyes seem blind because we cannot see the light of His mercy; when our hearts seem heavy because we cannot truly rejoice in the reward our sister has earned; in this hour when the meaning of death seems inscrutable: before us lies the answer to our question. We have found a virtuous woman who in her youth taught the little children in an ignorant community, who bore children out of her love for life, who served her community and her church with a loving heart. I say we have seen virtue and we come to honor this woman, Naomi Starr Foreman, whose life has been a sweet example for all who knew her. Yet in storms and lone . . ."

Coin's eyes hit Miss Horwitz. She sat there with her lips trembling in a sneer, opening and snapping the purse shut. He wished she'd order Reverend Brooks to stop because he was making people murmur all over the church. Small amens ran through the seats up to Reverend Brooks and when a loud one burst out he talked louder. Miss Horwitz had to make him stop! His father had his handkerchief out and he wiped his eyes more and more. If his father really began to cry, he couldn't bear it. He'd run out and go home. The tune snapped on in his head. *"We have no bananas today, we have no bananas today . . ."*

He must have been in a trance because when he woke up Reverend Brooks was speaking quiet and Coin knew he'd be finished soon.

"I wish in closing to say a word or two to the bereaved family and especially to Agnes, the oldest, upon whose shoulders the burden and joy of being another mother for these children has fallen. Remember always the example of patience and Christian charity your mother set before you. And children, obey your sister as you did your mother. To Deacon Foreman: I know your faith in the Lord will carry you through these hours of trial. We have found and known a virtuous woman. She is not sealed in this coffin, she has already arisen and is in our midst like a star to guide us. Naomi Starr . . ."

And he leaned over the pulpit, looked down at the casket.

". . . Naomi Starr, your spirit is among us but we shall miss you. We shall miss you. This country mourns your loss and says farewell. This state of New York mourns your loss and says farewell. This County of Kings in the Borough of Brooklyn mourns your loss and says farewell. . . ."

He paused and looked over the whole congregation.

"Naomi Starr Foreman, this church, the Corinthian Baptist Church of Christ, mourns your loss and says farewell. . . ."

The congregation replied like a choir chanting together, "Farewell!"

"And further, your family bids you goodbye and farewell. Your husband bids you farewell. . . ."

Popa's head fell on Agnes and his voice was thick and hoarse, "Goodbye, Naomi, goodbye, goodbye." He straightened up, blew his nose and was quiet as if nothing had happened.

". . . your children bid you goodbye and the farewell."

There was no response.

"I say your children bid you goodbye and the farewell."

It was a signal for a low moan through the church. Mrs. Quick was on hand. Coin knew he was expected to say the words but his throat burned and the tune went crazy in his head. Bananas were mixed with farewell. The organ started vibrating; he could feel it in his behind. Woody was crying on his shoulder. Bernice shouted in her high voice, her dark arm thrust up, shooting words in the air, "Goodbye, Mama, goodbye; don't leave me, don't leave me, Mama, Mama. Don't leave me alone."

She wept the same doomsday crying Agnes did three days ago. The congregation leaned forward in a body as Mrs. Quick rushed to the rescue. Agnes turned around, lifted her veil.

"Bernice, Bernice. Now, now."

"Nobody but Mama wants me, nobody," Bernice sang.

"I'll tend to her," Mrs. Quick told Agnes.

Reverend Brooks's hands went up, the black, birdwing, sleeves spread out, an eagle flying over the casket to carry it up to God's nest; he stood on tiptoe to finish, ". . . and I says, farewell."

The organ swelled up: *When the Roll Is Called Up Yonder, I'll Be There*. Sister Elba Fuller led the procession of the Dorcas Society down the left aisle. She carried stalks of wheat in either arm. She held her head high leading the singing. The other sisters marched behind her three by three, rocking from side to side, tramping to the tune. Some were crying with their heads held high and no veils to hide their tears. Coin could feel the rocking under his feet. Most of them were old with gray hair and white hair, many had shaking hands. They came weeping most pitifully as if it was their own funeral they were living through.

Seeing this, all notes of the banana tune left him and he was caught up in the solemn meaning of age and death and the mournful celebration of them.

When the trumpet of the Lord shall sound
And time shall be no more,
And the morning breaks eternal bright and fair,
When the saved of earth shall gather
To their home beyond the sky,
When the roll is called up yonder, I'll be there.

Sister Fuller's voice was a trumpet piercing the church above all the singing to break the stained-glass window. All the glass would shatter down colors, letting winter sunshine in. The old sisters just rocked in their white dresses, their black badges swayed from side to side. The whole church took up the refrain.

When the roll is called up yonder,
When the roll is called up yonder,
When the roll is called up yonder,
When the roll is called up yonder, I'll be there.

The society was grouped about the casket and each sister held the stalk of wheat Sister Fuller handed them. The congregation ceased singing and clapped the rhythm out low. Softly now the Dorcas Society sang another verse.

> *On that bright and cloudless morning*
> *When the saints of God shall rise*
> *And the glory of His resurrection share,*
> *When His chosen ones shall gather*
> *To their home beyond the skies,*
> *When the roll is called up yonder,*
> *I'll be there.*

Again the congregation took up the refrain. Men sang the bass till the church seemed to rock from side to side and the enormous chandelier rocked with it. Then each line got softer and softer. And when the last, "*When the roll is called up yonder, I'll be there,*" was sung, it was in a scared whisper.

In silence Sister Fuller laid her stalks of wheat on the casket, paused a second with a raised hand, moved to the head, and laid one hand on the coffin.

"These sheaves of wheat is the sign that life, life keeps on growing. Life will grow from thee, our dear sister, for you have set your days before us as a sample and as an example. You will grow in our hearts until the trumpet calls us all, and we go marching home together."

Her voice rose sharp, rose trembling, rose so high and triumphant, Coin felt a shiver up his spine.

She began the exit march up the right aisle. The others circled the casket laying their sheaves down, circling, singing.

> When the saints go marching home,
> Oh, when the saints go marching home,
> Lord, I want to be in that number,
> When the saints go march . . .

Their faces were set, their steps firm, their tears dry. For a moment Coin was convinced that they would march right out of the church and mount a gangplank up the air and through the clouds.

Agnes put one arm around Popa's shoulder.

> Oh, Lord, I want to be in that number,
> When the saints go marching home.

Reverend Brooks beckoned Undertaker Ward who came up, removed the flowers and wheat from the casket, opened the lid, adjusted inside, stepped to the foot end. He raised his right hand to the left side of the congregation. As the music of *The Master Went Alone to Pray* sounded, half the people stood and, guided by the undertaker's men, passed by to review the remains. They always said "the remains" as if everything wasn't in the casket.

Sister Sarah Russell sang quietly like a bird at night in a mysterious woods.

> *The master went alone to pray,*
> *Upon a twilight hill,*
> *He gathered strength before the day,*
> *Then moved among the throng to say:*
> *Oh, fretful tongues be still.*

Esther and her mother passed by with the others. Her mother had a scarf around her head fastened underneath the chin. She paused a long time. Esther touched his sleeve as she went up the aisle.

> *So let us find our hills of prayer*
> *Before we lose our way,*
> *Within a labyrinth of care,*
> *Before the mazes of despair*
> *Have led our hearts astray.*

The left side finished, Undertaker Ward raised his hand to the right side. Some people looked long and some looked short. Most of the old were crying. Some children didn't want to look and were forced to; some older boys and girls passed by without looking at all. Sister Russell sang on.

> *Let us dear Lord be stilled by Thee,*
> *Whenever we complain,*
> *And when a cross gains mastery*
> *Then let the shape of Calvary*
> *Loom tall beside our pain.*

The deacons and deaconesses filed by next. Deaconesses Redmond and Westerfield stood so long looking, Undertaker Ward touched them. Deaconess Westerfield came and knelt by Coin's pew, put her arm around him. The old feeling of wanting to touch the hump, for good luck, almost got hold of him.

It was time for the family to see for the last time. Aunt Harriet went first, supported by Mrs. Quick. She stood there, lifted her veil and came back with her hands to her face. Undertaker Ward helped Uncle Troy.

The master went alone at eve,
Yet always came again . . .

The whole church stretched forward to see a blind man look goodbye to his sister. Uncle Troy's hand went into the casket, probably touching the face as he had touched Coin's at the station. When he turned around tears were streaming out of his eyes, staring blind ahead. He dropped his stick and groped for it. Undertaker Ward attended to that.

Woody, Oscar and Bernice, with Mrs. Quick attending, went together. Deaconess Westerfield was urging Coin to please go. He shook his head no and no and no.

When Agnes got up, Miss Horwitz was there to help her. She glanced inside, started away and went back. She searched inside, up and down, and came away dry-eyed, but as she sat down with her veil raised Coin thought she and Miss Horwitz looked like a picture he had seen in the Sunday school lesson of Mary and Martha at the foot of the cross.

Popa shook his head no, when the time came for him. Coin was staring at the cardboard clock in the round wreath of flowers, with the hands set to the time his mother died. He thought he heard a ticking flat and soft. The long hand slipped. His mother died at nine-thirty instead of ten o'clock.

Deaconess Westerfield had persuaded him. Her voice had almost reached a whispered command. He allowed himself to be led. Deacon Fuller lifted him up, bending his head down.

> . . . *we have no bananas today,*
> *We have no bananas today* . . .

Coin shook his head from side to side to get the tune out. He opened his screwed-up eyes and gazed in a long time. He couldn't take his eyes away. A magician, the one that had come to school once, must have tricked up the thing in the casket they said was his mother. The face was sunk into the pillow making hard double chins. Under the pale brown of her skin there was a purple color and the lips were squeezed together like she was angry (she was never angry), the balls of her eyes looked stuffed under the skin (she smiled with her eyes), her cheeks were touched with red and the powder was peeling (she never put that stuff on). He screamed when he saw her hands: one clutched the other fiercely. He yelled out.

"That's not my mother, that's not my mother, that's not my mother, that's not Mama. Mama, Mama, Mama." The tears came swift and hot, blinding his eyes to the body. That was his mother and that's what death looked like. His tears would never stop. Deacon Fuller pulled him away. He fell down by his father's knees.

When the procession went out, Mr. Foreman had to carry Coin.

On the way to the cemetery nobody spoke. Bernice was knotted up in the back seat corner like one of her old dolls with eyes closed and long black lashes quivering every once in a while when the wind spoke through the slit of open window. It was cold and white outside as the Cadillac rushed to meet the five o'clock cemetery deadline. If they didn't arrive in time the gates would be closed. For once Woody had no comment to make on anything. He was riding with the driver and his eyes followed the wheel. Uncle Troy had his arm around Coin. And Miss Horwitz, who had no order to keep, stared ahead. In a way Coin was scared. The road was slippery. Once the car slipped to the edge of the road at left and to the edge of the road at right. There was danger but nobody noticed and he wouldn't, and he couldn't speak the story he heard the deaconesses talking about in the dining room that morning. Mrs. Clovis had died and on the way to her cemetery in the cold, in the ice and snow the drivers had gone so fast the hearse went over the edge. The first car with Mr. Clovis in it had been wrecked. He was buried the next week beside his wife. The deaconesses said that Mrs. Clovis' casket rolled down a hillside in a mess of mud. "Must have shook her up a good deal," said Deaconess Redmond.

The Cadillac jerked out of line as it reached the gates. Miss Horwitz spoke for the first time. "I don't know why I came out here with an incompetent driver to be scared half to death."

"I'm doing the best I can, lady; these roads ain't no holiday."

The cemetery bells began to toll. Back and forth they

gonged in the air. Coin heard them faintly even at the grave.

The tall finger trees were full with snow. Everywhere was white except the family ranged around the grave, black crying birds against the sky. Each had been given one flower. As Reverend Brooks said the ashes to ashes and dust to dust, one by one they tossed the flowers on top of the casket, deep in the hole. Coin's carnation hit the box with a little sound he'd always remember. Uncle Troy's iris landed in snow in the opposite direction. Undertaker Ward picked it up and threw it in the grave. Coin turned his uncle the right way. The men with shovels dug into a waiting pile of hard dirt and thump by thump they started filling. Deep, deep down in Coin's mind the idea of leaving his mother there, in the cold hole, made a knotted pain in his throat. The thump, thump, thump, thumps seemed like knocking from inside the casket. Wanting to get out, get warm, he clutched his uncle's hand harder, but he wanted to run away and bury himself where the sound couldn't reach, where his eyes couldn't see shovels of dirt thrown on the box his mother was in. Thump, thump, thump. No one answered. The flowers they had thrown were all covered: roses, irises, carnations, ferns and the rest. His mother's closed eyes and the hands clutching each other were awaiting the final resurrection from the frozen grave. The pages of Reverend Brooks's Bible fluttered in the wind. His breath came out in stiff clouds. The finger trees bent, shedding their snow.

As they went back to the cars there was no sound. From the Cadillac, Coin watched the men pile flowers on top of the filled-up hole. The clock wreath was last but the purple clock with the white hands was gone. There was only a doughnut hole where time had been.

How it had happened, he never knew. Only Uncle Troy, still holding his hand, was in the car with him. The other three were somewhere else. Coin was glad for that. For a long time neither spoke. Darkness sped down. They were closed in. The headlights from the Cadillac searched ahead for safety.

Uncle Troy reached in his great coat pocket and brought out a pint bottle.

"It's colder than the grave in here, son, ain't it," and Uncle Troy took a long drink, bubbling and gurgling. His eyes seemed to bore holes in the top of the car.

Colder than the grave. They said she wouldn't know the cold; she was waiting for Beulah land. That was the mystery he couldn't bear. How could she arise and be the same when she wasn't the same when he saw her? Only now he saw her as they used to be in the house alone together. "Coin, fasten my corset here," or "Coin, meet your father at the station tonight with this umbrella; it's raining cats and dogs outside," or "Coin, tell me what you did in school today." And he'd answer and she'd say, "You'll get to college yet, the Lord willing and the devil don't object." He saw her plain, plainer than Uncle Troy licking his lips. If he could see her like that as he went along, then he might forget what was left in the grave.

"I said, it's colder than the grave in here, son, ain't it. You wasn't listening."

"No, sir."

"Sir! You know, boy, that's the first in a long time that I been sired."

"No, sir."

"You like to travel, son?"

"Yes, sir."

"I'm glad you do. Now that I been sired three times you can call me Uncle Troy again."

He would have to go home. He would have to travel home. That was the only travel he could do. He'd sleep across from the empty bed. The bosses would be Agnes and Miss Horwitz.

The headlights of the car reached into the tunnel of night. Tonight when he lay down to sleep there would be a tunnel with no light. Nothing.

"What do you do summers, Coin?"

"Nothing."

"You got any plans?"

"No, Uncle Troy."

"You're a good boy. Almost the spit and image of Naomi. I want you to be good until summer. Will you do that?"

"Yes, sir."

"Do you know what, boy?"

"What?"

"Your mother was the salt of the earth. Are we almost home?"

"We're at Atlantic and Pennsylvania."

"You sure got an eye to business."

Uncle Troy took the bottle out again. As he put it away, he put his arm around Coin. Coin felt better already. Maybe he would take him for a walk tomorrow to see Mr. Jeffers. Mr. Jeffers had a bottle, too.

AFTER Uncle Troy left every sound almost was connected with the train that would carry him to Washington, D. C., when school was out, to guide the blind around the city with chewing gum and pencils. All the rest of the winter geography lesson, with Miss Raidin, was the best class. Of course, they never studied much about Washington, the capital of the United States. But just the knowledge that he would be on trains and see strange places, that he would soon be away from Agnes' frown and Miss Horwitz, talking a hole in his head, from the church sisters' sorrowing for him and the house he slept in and ate in but didn't belong in any longer; just the knowledge made him feel wild and roaming, happy for geography. He felt he would be going farther than Washington someday: to India or China where everyone had a laundry and was so clean no flies could find a leftover to eat; to Italy to see Mrs. Renaldo's house where she was born and squeeze olive oil from trees Caesar had planted.

Oh, he was going. The El trains roaring down Pitkin Avenue roared his dream from station to station, every five minutes.

Once in a while when he was in the house and Agnes was working he would try to get back to the old way of being with his mother. He would ask, "Can I help you?"

"No, Coin. You're hanging around the house today. It's cold out but you won't freeze. You don't want to be a sissy, do you?"

"No, Agnes."

"Then go out and play like a regular boy."

"I always helped Mama."

"Mama needed your help. I don't."

"I'll go out and play, Agnes."

"That's a good boy."

He felt the knife in her voice cutting him. He would never offer again. Fartsafongoo forever on her.

Once, when the weather was warm, he heard Agnes and Miss Horwitz crying together because Harry had gone away. It was all because the children were there and how could he marry Agnes if he had to marry the whole family. Miss Horwitz had said, "You ought to put the children in an orphanage and live your own life."

"I promised Mama I'd take care of them. I promised her, I promised. And Popa needs me. He's been so far away since the funeral. We haven't talked much. He gives me his check and asks nothing. He's lonely."

"Oh," Miss Horwitz had answered, "I wouldn't worry about your pious father; he's taking care of himself all right."

"No, he's gotten thinner. He doesn't even smoke his cigars on the sly any more. He hasn't begun to plant the back yard. He's waiting for something. Lucy, I love him; I want to be here but I need . . . Harry . . . I . . . oh, I don't know."

"I wish I could talk some sense into your head," Miss Horwitz had replied, taking off her pinch-glasses and rubbing her upper nose. "Your precious father finds plenty to do in his spare time. Where do you think he goes after supper every night since it's been mild? Ask anybody. Sitting in Highland Park just as brazen as brass . . ."

"No, Lucy. That's not true."

"Huh!" was Miss Horwitz' sound, "men stink. I wouldn't trust one of them farther than I could throw them."

Your breath stinks, thought Coin, you buttermilk. He reviewed the words in his mind when he slipped away. He felt guilty for hearing so much. He felt guilty being in the way, longed for magic to trick himself out of their sight. Woody didn't need magic; he just wandered the streets all day after school in his long pants and came in anytime to sleep. Bernice was forever at some girl friend's house reading and studying so she could graduate and get a job. Oscar was reforming in reform school. Coin couldn't always be away from the house, so he heard many things and got scoldings. If he caught them talking about him, they didn't even stop, they went right on, as if he never hurt inside.

"Well, anyway," Agnes had said once toward the end of June, "as soon as school is out, Coin will be in Washington with Uncle Troy. I got a letter from him last week."

"That's one less mouth to feed," Miss Horwitz had chimed in.

At that moment Coin had been at the door. They looked up at him.

"You'll enjoy stuffing yourself with nobody around to say you may, won't you, Coin?" Miss Horwitz had laughed her stink at him.

"I don't know, Miss Horwitz," he had answered. She had been so nice to him when he was little. She was nice to all the children on the block before they could talk good. Then one morning she'd curse one out she'd given a lollypop and take a new favorite in the afternoon.

As June neared only the sound of the train was important and he and Esther wandered and explored.

When they were together, he didn't think hard. Esther suggested that they start a butterfly collection. Chris O'Connor came in too, and Davey Carth, who had become a friend since his mother's funeral. They ran wild all over Highland Park, casting homemade nets in the bright spring air, trapping flower butterflies. At night they pinned them on cardboard covered with cotton and examined the colors in the designs. Esther knew all the names both in English and in science. She would consult her book, *Our Wonder World*, and come up with the right answer every time.

"Look, this wing is the color of the sky. Here's one with a rainbow," Esther pointed, "this wing has sunshine."

"Here," Chris said, "is a baby one."

"Butterflies," Esther looked at him sharp as Miss Binatree, "have no childhood. It says so right here."

"Aw, that's a lie, Esther," Chris wanted to show off. "I seen little and big butterflies and moths, too; I don't care what any old book says."

"In the book it says: 'The butterfly has, in a sense, no childhood, certainly no parental care. At each stage as it emerges. . . !' "

"What's 'emerges'?"

"Listen, Mr. Smartie, and you'll see. 'At each stage it emerges, first as a caterpillar, then as butterfly, it is able to take complete care of itself.' There it is written down and if you don't believe it, write a book yourself." Esther closed *Our Wonder World* and smiled at each one of them. Coin stared at the butterflies pinned down. In a second he smiled faintly back at Esther.

The day he found out that Miss Horwitz was wrong about his father was chilly for June. He didn't wear much extra; he'd be running anyhow to heat up. Just after supper he and Chris rounded up Davey and ran almost all the way to the park, then separated to find the treasure Esther said she had hidden: "where the weather gets coldest, where the sun begins and near a bush tree." Coin thought he knew the place already. Esther had given him hints. She hadn't really cheated. Just hints. He ran in the direction. Chris and Davey would be thrown off the track looking for a bush tree. Bush tree meant the tree where the squirrels with the bushiest tails hid their food. It was near the east reservoir and had a bench around the trunk. Running into the wind made him feel he was sailing through space; perhaps he was a bird. Up the hill, toward the tree, he flew, then rested behind a nearby gingko. After a minute he looked around to make sure the kids weren't coming, then sneaked nearer the bush one. There was a man on the bench. That made him mad. Sitting on his treasure. Coin wanted to shoo him away, but when he looked again he saw it was his father very still on the edge of the seat. For the first time since his mother died, he looked hard at his father. His face was gray and his hair was grayer and he stared straight ahead. He only had his body coat on in this chilly weather. As Coin walked to the bench he saw that his father held the paper rose Mama had thrown to him on the day of the block party.

"Hello, Popa."

"Hello, son."

They sat awhile in silence.

"Popa, it's getting cold."

"Yes, it is, son," his father answered, thrusting the rose into his pocket, "I think maybe we ought to stop by Grant's Ice Cream parlor for some hot chocolate to warm us up. Yes, sir-re-Bob, that's what we'll have to do."

From that moment his father seemed alive to him again. His eyes lit up as he took his hand and they walked down the hill. The treasure was forgotten and Coin didn't speak. He wouldn't spoil his father's mood as Agnes had done last month when Popa pulled up to the table saying, "Dinner money, who gets it?" his voice had been loud and round, jolly. Woody and Bernice, home on time for dinner for once, made big grins.

Agnes had snapped, "You know very well who gets it."

The dinner had been eaten in silence. Popa didn't speak again, not even for a second helping.

Now, walking beside him, Coin would not say a word but held his father's hand tighter and his father commenced humming in return.

Sitting in the ice cream parlor made him recall the time when he had planned miracles and his mother walked home lame. The thought came to his mind as he blew on the whipped cream heaped on the hot chocolate that there were no miracles except in the movies. Somebody or other could tell you how everything worked. Even magic had a book explaining all secrets bare. Plans you made broke in half, too, most of the time, like crackers, and if you tried to mend them some important crumb was lost. He would be leaving for Washington and he determined not to expect too much. It was good enough that he would be going another place and guiding a hand that loved him. He glanced at his father drinking slowly and felt closer to him than ever before. They were both in the same boat. Agnes had on the Captain's cap.

"Son, I hope you'll be happy in Washington. I want you to write me often and if you want to come home, just write that too."

"Yes, sir."

"I know you'll miss your brother. Well, we can't be together always. We all have to leave those dear to us. . . ."

As his father talked, Coin drank faster, knowing that the voice was directed only partly to him but mostly it seemed to be wandering in some lonesome place and the echo of it sang back a million years old. Gray voice, echo voice, white hairs in the voice.

"I wish there was a way we could tell one another what mistakes will come and how to do. There is no way, son. I wish you didn't have to start out so early. I know you will see things and feel things you won't understand. Pray. Sometimes just saying things out loud makes trouble and joy clearer. No one can show you the way, Coin. You find that alone. Momps . . . your mother . . ."

That was the first time he had mentioned her name since the funeral.

". . . your mother might have been your shield and buckler had she lived. Verses from the Bible are signs but mostly you seek alone. That's growing up."

Coin felt his forehead wrinkling up and his upper lip reach his nose. He looked into the dusty mirror behind the counter. He was not used to this kind of talk from Popa. He laughed suddenly so as not to cry, even though he listened carefully to all his father said. He knew he would never forget the words. Mr. Foreman watched him as he laughed. He stopped talking; his face was like it had been in the park; his eyes stared ahead like he was staring into solid blackness. Coin could have whipped himself.

"Popa," he burst out, "Popa, I was listening, honest, I was. I'll remember everything you said. I was only laughing because, because . . ." His father's hand was over his mouth.

"That's all right, son. I was speaking like you were grown. I forgot you were still a boy. It's time to go home, I reckon."

Mr. Foreman gave a deep sigh. There was whipped cream on his heavy mustache. Coin decided not to mention it.

The hand shook his shoulder in three hard jerks.

"Coin," Agnes whispered, "it's time to get up. You're leaving this morning, you know."

Automatically he looked across at the bed where his

father was sleeping, dead to the world. Woody, by his side, snored like an engine. The whole house was asleeping on his going-away morning.

"And don't wake anybody up. It's too early. And it's you that's going, not them. I'll fix breakfast while you wash and dress."

Leaving. Since he had heard the news, leaving had seemed the happiest word he knew. *Leaving*. It was a word you could stretch when you said it. It wasn't like *don't*. But now, looking at every familiar crack in the walls, with his spyglass eyes, and the splotches in the ceilings, at everything he had known since he could remember, leaving was walking off a gangplank into the geography ocean and getting tangled in all the lines of longitude and latitude; lost in the cities stamped in hard black letters; crying in the jigsaw countries, the islands of dots; lonesome in the Alps, without his mother in the valleys or the stinking words Miss Horwitz said or the knuckles of Agnes in his side, the red laughter of Woody, the smell of his father's clothes, the ghosts of the cats he had buried, the freckles of Esther, the hole the nail made at the door for his mother's crepe, Miss Raidin's perfume, the small shriek of Miss Van Epps's harmonica. Leaving was a bandit word with black eyes, with a gun for a nose, with Agnes at the trigger.

Leaving. Was he ever coming back? Agnes said, "Maybe for school. Or if you like it down there, you can even stay." They didn't want him back. He was menaced to stay down there.

"*Leaving.*" The sounds he whispered made him stone cold in the warm bed.

"Coin, get up this minute or I'll know the reason why."

"I'm up, Agnes."

Throwing the covers off, he stepped into the bathroom to run his bath. Once in the tub, he let the water sneak up his body. If he let it run long enough it would be into his mouth, ears and eyes, into a drown. He bubbled. The lukewarm thawed him out gradually. He worked his toes and splashed gently with his hands and then faster and faster.

"Coin!"

"Yes, Agnes."

"Stop that!" She had opened the door. Quickly he covered himself with the washcloth and was confused because he had never done that before. He had never thought of it before and didn't know why he did now.

With the door ajar, the smell of bacon drifted in. He heard the eggbeater going. Hot rolls were in the air. He pulled the stopper out and began drying himself real fast.

Pennsylvania Station was no surprise to him since he had been there to meet Uncle Troy. Now he was going to meet him again. The porter went ahead with his bag and he and Agnes followed him into the train. The bag was overhead on the shelf, his lunch was on the seat beside him. He held onto the box containing his share of the pinned butterflies Esther had given him last night.

The final thing Agnes did was to tie a tag to the second button of his coat with his name, where he was going and who to get in touch with in case.

"Coin," Agnes said, "take good care of yourself, write us and I'll write back all the news. Give my love to Uncle Troy." There was nothing else to say; she had said just about everything in the last two weeks. As the train moved through the tunnel, Coin still felt Agnes' flat kiss on his cheek.

As soon as the train shot out of the tunnel, Coin decided it was time to eat his lunch. At least Agnes had fixed him up swell. There was enough for now and later on. He bit into a ham sandwich and gazed out on the twisting roads and the fields of ashes and garbage. In the distance through a haze he saw the skyline of New York. He thought it would be strange but it was like the pictures he knew. He felt more comfortable because he recognized it. As people bustled up and down the aisles they smiled at him. Sometimes it was hard with his jaws full to smile back. When he was thirsty he tried the water fountain. When he had to do number one he found the door. He flushed his water below on the running ground. Railroad tracks must stink. Whew!

The time passed looking at his butterflies and the spring outside rushing by. White blooming trees and water pushing under bridges with the sun in the foam. There were fields and fields of black dirt turned up ready for seeds, corn maybe, tomatoes and lettuce. The sound of the train wheels could be put to any words. A rhythm underneath rocked him to sleep against the plush seat.

"CHESTER, CHESTER, the next stop is CHESTER," the conductor rolled the word out. He made Chester seem like a capital. When the train stopped, it was at an old station. A red sign announced Chester again and that was all except a lot of colored people got on there and most of them pushed right into the car where Coin was. They were dressed up and laughing to beat the band. One great bosom lady sat across from him with her son. He was peaked and looked like the last rose of summer. Kept on calling her Ma. Kept hugging her up. A fat old boy was in the seat in front of the woman. He called her Mama. Others took seats here and there and commenced to yelling and waving and passing bottles and sandwiches. It was a picnic on the train. When the conductor came by for the tickets, there was such a digging into pockets and paper bags and wallets, looking under seats and acting the fool until all the tickets were handed in to screaming laughter. Coin began to laugh too, whenever someone said anything funny. They kept on saying funny things and he kept on laughing. The train heated up until you could hardly breathe. Smelled like outing flannel and asafoetida. You weren't supposed to open the windows. Coin got himself cold water three times. When he was coming back the last time the talking and jokes and eating was louder and whooped-up more than ever. A man at the front of the car rose up out of his seat a little and called back, "Why don't you darkies shut up so we kin hear ourselves think."

What did he want to say that for? The happy confusion died down to a silence like an axe was hanging overhead by a thread. It stayed that way for a long time. Only the train wheels still raced: why don't you darkies shut up, why don't you darkies shut up.

The bosom woman's bosom panted up and down. She took three long puffs of her cigarette letting the smoke out of her nose in straight clouds, then she stood up, scrubbing the butt into the floor carefully. This woman, who had talked so hard and eaten more chicken than six, who had a laugh like a ten-gun salute, began walking down the aisle toward the man who had asked for silence. As she trod, she seemed to grow tall and furious as one of Popa's Bible prophets, Moses maybe or Genesis. You could see it in her back, in the way she threw her shoulders and lifted her head. People around buzzed low like the sound of bees with special stings. She reached her destination, leaned over the seat and pointed one dagger finger.

"If you don't know what you're talking about, you'd better ask somebody." Her voice filled the car and drowned the sound of the wheels.

"Nuts," came out of the seat, "nuts, you folks keeping up enough racket to drive a man crazy."

"You don't need to be driv crazy. You crazy already, that's what you are. Don't you come calling me no darkie."

"Aw, lady."

"Don't you be calling me no lady either. I been bringing up your children and scrubbing your nasty houses until my bones fair ache inside me. I ain't no lady, I'm a truck horse. Been a truck horse for you for too many years and I'm too tired to listen to you shutting me up. You hear that."

A voice from somewhere said, "NIGGERS, niggers," and that was all.

"Who said that!" She shot around and her eyes blazed fire even to where Coin sat. "You ain't afraid to say it again, is you? Cowards. That's what you is, a coward. Niggers, niggers. My boy is lying in the fields of Europe on the Kaiser's acres, that's where he is and I got a medal from the government. Cowards. It's too bad they didn't get your ass, that's what's too bad." She looked left and right, high and low. Only the train wheels dared to make a noise. Finally she strode back to her seat. Her heavy body seemed to shake the train. When she took her seat again, the boy who called her Mama turned around.

"Keep quiet, Mama, keep your big mouth shut."

She faced him like the wrath of God.

"Keep quiet, keep quiet! Why you shoulda been down there instead of me. Keep quiet, you chicken, that's what you is. Nobody's gonna call me out of my name. You hear me!" She worked herself up again. She walked up the aisle and down the aisle being bumped first to one side and then the other. Her voice sounded the hallelujah Sister Maudesta Lee shouted in church.

"All the planes that were fallen, and the ships rammed

into, the bombs splitting the ocean apart, poison gas. God has a way."

The train wheels sang between her silences. People looked down.

"Don't give us nothing. Stepping all over us. Calling us darkies and niggers. God has a way. Colored boys working in the manholes of the streets in Philadelphia 'cause a white boy got his head rammed off by a trolley car. God has a way. They put colored on after that. Colored boys crawling about like cats under the streets and don't look out of them holes lessen they look both ways. They smart. God has a way. Trying to spoil my holiday. Don't give but the one day and you calling me outta my name. I hope there comes a next war. I hope they knocks hell outta this country. That's what I hopes. You can't think. Well, you better think. The end of the world is scheduled to be by fire. Now, if you don't know what you're talking about, you'd better keep quiet." She paused. The sweat was running off of her forehead in beads. She sat down again like on a throne. The train wheels sounded but didn't say any words.

When the train pulled into Baltimore, the bosom woman and her friends got off. They stood at the window where the man who had asked them to keep quiet sat, gazed in long like at an animal in the zoo. As the train started again, they all laughed at him; laughed pure and long and solid. The train wheels took up the laughter. It lasted almost until Washington.

Coin knew something was wrong with the way everyone had acted but he didn't know where to place the blame. One thing he had learned: what nobody would tell him. He knew now what a nigger was. His mother really had been right. A bad person. What confused him was that it meant much more than that. Maybe you weren't a bad person but you were colored and they called you nigger.

Walking with the rest of the people toward the exit, Coin spied Uncle Troy at the gate. He was so happy to see him that he broke into a trot calling his name.

"Uncle Troy."

"Coin, Coin!"

"Uncle Troy."

Coin rushed to him and his uncle felt his face, measured his height with his stick.

"Lord, boy, I thought a baby was coming here to me but you're almost grown. Must have grown several inches since I saw you. Let me look at you." His hands felt Coin's face, and the old laughter Coin remembered from Pennsylvania Station surrounded them. "Well, you might as well begin working now. Mrs. Walker brought me here but gotta lead me there." He was still laughing as Coin took his hand. The porter brought Coin's bag and hailed a taxi for them.

In the cab Uncle Troy began to laugh again.

"What's this I feel on your chest?"

"Agnes put a tag on me."

"Now isn't that just like Agnes, sending you like freight."

WHEN he first entered the Gem Movie Playhouse, on Seventh Street, the darkness reminded him of underwater and deep periods of sleep and down in the damp cellar on Berriman Street. He thought of the woods, near Atkins Avenue, with trees at the top spreading, long branches shaking hands and all the birds you could hardly ever see. The kids called them the up-in-the-tree birds. Now it was brighter and he felt alone, more alone than ever, with kids everywhere. In his remembered woods he saw a squirrel leap from branch to branch in the nanny goat lady's oak tree. He wished the animal would hop to him. Come to him like on the day his mother died, the sparrow came and he knew the chirping was asking for crumbs. He bit his left thumbnail off and placed it between his two front teeth and worked it in and out there. He slid down into his seat and looked at the silver screen. Tom Mix raced along low slopes toward a sign that read EL PASO. He caught up a girl riding on the behind of the bad guy's horse. A whole flock of men waited in the distance with guns. Then all of a sudden a shot banged out of the piano in the front of the theatre and the bad guy's horse's front legs hit up in the air kicking. The pretty girl slid down the slick behind of the horse like on a slide in the playground and she was on a cactus plant crying to beat the band. Coin let out a long ahhhhh geeeeeeeee. That was when he noticed the boy beside him.

"That's all right," said the boy, "it's only a picture; it ain't real."

"Yeah," said Coin. But it was realer than that and he wanted to help the girl up and bring some iodine. Iodine all over her arms and behind. It wasn't real, that's right, he thought. And Rudolph Valentino wasn't real. "Valentino was dead living on the silver screen," Mrs. Jeffers had said last summer between her crying. So now he knew. And he knew the boy realized the same thing, so he answered, "Yeah, yeah, I know that."

When the lights went on he smelled the perfume like toilet smell and baby talcum powder mixed. He wanted to rush into fresh air. A big bag of peanuts was thrust under his nose and he took a handful as the seat snapped up and the kids began to rush out in scrambled talk, piano pounding and giggling. The boy at his side asked, "You goin' out or stayin' for the next show?"

"I'm goin'. I gotta wait for my uncle."

In the light outside the movie he sneaked a look at the boy. He was older than him. His hair grew forward and his eyes were real black and white, like the color black had been separated from the white by a jacknife. The boy's face shone. Not greasy but the leaping shiny of autos. His fingers looked strong and hard as he asked Coin to have some more peanuts.

"Fillin'. Almost a meal, that's what peanuts is. Peanuts is the best thing in Washington, District of Columbia." And he cocked his head from side to side and began a smile that showed laughing teeth. "This Washington ain't the other Washington, the state. Teacher said so."

"Yeah," said Coin twisting his face on a sour peanut. Probably one of Mrs. Carth's. He smiled too. They were both smiling at each other and Coin couldn't stop.

"Can't you say nothin' but yeah?" the boy asked Coin.

"Yeah. What's your name?"

"That's more like it. Whoever ain't got the grit to talk ain't from nothin' or nowhere. My name's Ferris."

"I ain't heard of no name like that."

"Well, that's my name. Ferris. I was named after the wheel, Ferris wheel. Sometimes I feel like a wheel too, feel like I'm goin' round and round up and down. I can turn a cartwheel, too."

"Ferris sounds made up."

"A Ferris wheel got lights on it. Lights in a ball of glass. Seen 'em in a carnival in Kentucky. A big ring lighted in the sky. Music, too. When my Mama was carryin' me she was ridin' the wheel. That's how come my name."

"Your Mama took a baby up in them swingin' seats?"

"That was before I was born."

"She couldn't have been carryin' you then."

"Yes, she was. My Mama was."

"Not before you were born."

"You don't know from nothin'. How you suppose babies is made?"

"Well, you know," Coin answered vaguely. He bit a peanut loud. "Say, Ferris, look at that big airplane flying up there. It looks like a grasshopper with double wings."

"Hey, hey all over. Look at that big airplane," Ferris repeated. "Don't you know babies is carried?"

"Sure I do."

"You do! Then tell me if you're so knowing." Coin just shuffled along and looked like he was interested in the sky and the airplane that was out of sight. But Ferris kept at it like rubbing in sandpaper. All Coin could think of was that he was delivered when he was born. He looked slantways at Ferris and thought, old country boy. He don't know from doodley-squat!

Ferris began to laugh sharp and gooey like an eggbeater going.

"Don't you know all carry their young. Except some birds. They lay 'em in eggs."

"Uh huh," Coin managed to say.

"Furthermore, do you know how babies is conceived?"

"Conceived?"

"Began and started, boy you is the dumbest boy this side Kentucky."

They had reached a small park, surrounded by stores and houses, where hardly anybody was.

Ferris sat down on the first bench and kept on talking. "Babies is made from a man and a woman. I seen it. Man goes in and after the woman is fat for nine months, baby comes crying. That's the gist of it."

Coin had heard of that but he didn't believe babies came from it. He didn't come from nothing dirty like that. "My mother and father never did anything like that."

Ferris laughed. "How do you think you're here eatin' peanuts and talkin' to me?"

"My mother never did nothin' dirty like that and you better shut up. You better shut right up if you don't want a punch in your friggin' nose!" Coin felt hot all over like a blazing was inside him. He stood up over Ferris with fists clenched and tears in his eyes, muttering to the boy lying on the bench rolling with laughing. "You're a bastard, you're a bastard. Bastard, bastard. Double bastard. Get up and fight."

Ferris sat up quickly.

"Maybe your mother did that thing but mine never did. My mother's the salt of the earth. She was the salt . . ."

"Hey boy. Hey, hey." Ferris put his arms friendly

around Coin and Coin thrust him off. Ferris landed on the bench.

"I don't allow nobody to call me that. If you wanta fight, put 'em up. Put 'em up." Ferris' eyes were turning red as Coin talked.

Coin was shaking and sweat was on his forehead as a small group of boys began crowding, egging them on.

"Better knock him in the head before he gets up offa that bench."

"He's afraid: ha ha ha."

"They both sissies, that's what."

"Nobody better not call me no bastard." Ferris, growling like a dog, got to his feet and faced Coin. Coin hitched his knickers up and hitched them up again. Ferris narrowed his eyes. Then they stood dead still staring into each other's eyes.

One sideline kid shouted, "Shucks, ain't no use waitin', ain't no use waitin'. They both sissies."

Just then a fly began to tickle on Coin's nose and as he raised a hand to brush it off he felt a lam in his right eye and saw firecracker stars of all colors. Raising his fists to hit at Ferris, he tripped. His knickers had fallen down. Ferris was on top of him and he heard all the yelling children, felt blow after blow on his cheeks and chest. He knew he was a mess. When one sock of Ferris' went into his right eye, he saw a shooting star land and his mother's face came out of it. A blue face laughing and stars splintering in her hair. That was when he made force in his left arm and flinging it up gripped Ferris' head in a half-nelson. He heard his voice sputtering, "Do you give up, do you give up, do you give up?"

With every repeat of the phrase he locked Ferris' head tighter till he thought Ferris must be dead. They were both sweating and dirt scratched everywhere on Coin's body. His mother was sitting in the window and the little man of sunshine bowed and bowed over her white hair; he saw her face in the coffin with red stuff on the cheeks and the lips hugged close. Mama over the washtub and Mama inspecting him saying: get up get up get up before you get so dirty Popa will be mad. Mama and johnnycake. Ferris was still as nothing and the sideline boys were still but he asked the question, "How is babies born, how, how, how . . . no dirty, no dirty . . . ?"

Ferris' voice came at last as Coin released him, "Babies . . . ?"

"Take it all back!"

"Babies . . . is delivered," Ferris voice was panting. Through his sweat Coin looked at him close. Ferris' eyes began to get big.

"All right, all right," Coin said. "You give up?"

"I gives up."

With the excitement over the kids drifted away. Coin didn't know what to say. Ferris was over by the bench. He picked up the bag that had had peanuts in it, gathered it together at the top and blew hard. The bag puffed out. Taking it out of his mouth he twisted the ragged edges and popped the paper ball with his fist. Coin turned around to a smiling Ferris.

"There ain't, there ain't not even one peanut left."

They smoothed their clothes in silence and drank at a fountain. Ferris broke the silence first.

"I ain't asked you your name."

"Coin."

"Like a penny?"

"Yeah."

Ferris laughed until he bent over. "Whooooooo wheeeeee whooooo ummmmmmmm. That's the funniest yet. Why boy, you as bad as me in name."

"Yeah," grinned Coin.

Ferris whooped harder. He turned a cartwheel and yelled, "I'm gonna spend you boy." He ran along a path quick as hot cakes, quick as sixty and Coin was at his heels laughing with his nose running and the sunlight sharp in his hurting eyes but he didn't care.

At the edge of the park a man was ringing a Santa Claus bell, standing by a dirty white cart looking like who-struck-john. The boys stopped short. Ferris went over to the cart with bottles of all flavors in them and a big hunk of ice and a scooping cup.

"Coin, you like scraped ice and flavorin'?"

"Thanks."

"Don't ever say thanks till you get somethin' to thank for," said Ferris handing him a snowball of shaved ice with mint green flavoring.

"Ferris, you know, you're one of the nicest friends I ever had. You're the nicest."

"You know why? I was raised on a sugar tit."

"You ought to come by my room and meet my uncle. He's blind but he can really get around with that stick."

181

"Wish I could, Coin, but I gotta get to the station. Lord, that reminds me, what time do you reckon it is? Mister, what time is it?"

The man at the cart took an alarm clock from under his apron.

"Twenty minutes to six."

"What are you in such a big hurry for, Ferris?"

"I'm going home tonight, goin' to Kentucky. And I ain't gonna miss the seven o'clock train. I'm gonna scoot out of this Washington, District of Columbia, so fast the wind gonna wonder how I flew."

"I'm sorry you're leavin' . . . just when I found someb . . ." Coin couldn't swallow his last scraps of ice and he liked mint flavoring too. "Can I go to the station with you?"

"You better come. We can walk from here."

"How about your bag and things?"

"My Aunt Louise sent everything along ahead, before she went to work, and left a lunch box in the bag room. I got the ticket here."

"Lord," sighed Ferris as they walked along kicking stones and cans ahead, "Lord, I sure will be glad to get back. Wake up in the morning and it's so quiet and no noise to make you sick. Just before the sun come out, the birds commence to sing and by midday you can hardly bear it. Their music everywhere; catbirds, finches, little finches, redbirds, chickadees. Sure will be glad to get back. An fishin', too, in the crick. Stand sometime in quicksand . . ."

Coin's face was almost stuck under Ferris' mouth.

". . . of course I hold onto a branch. Sometimes gold minnows fairly blazin'. And sometimes I just lie down in the high grass and look up in the sky . . . look like a big old blue tent. Brush snake doctors away."

"What are snake doctors?"

"Boy, you don't know nothing. They flies that tend sick snakes. Got wings like glass when they fly in the sun. They pretty but they mean. I ain't scared of them though. Just lay down in the high grass and watch the clay hills, 'long about sunset, roll away like molassas puddin's."

"I can just see them."

"Lord, I hope that train fairly races. This city makes me nervous. All the autos. Jar me so. Feel like a bell ringin' in me."

Coin saw it all and wished he could just leave everybody and thing and get on that train with Ferris. And he could send for Esther maybe. Esther could teach both of them after regular school.

Ferris was singing:

> *Honey in the bee ball,*
> *I can't see ya'll.*
> *A bushel of ree,*
> *A bushel of rye,*
> *All that ain't hid*
> *On judgement day,*
> *Better holler I.*

"What's that, Ferris?"

"Hide-and-seek song."

"We play that all the time. Hide and go seek."

"Boy, don't cut out the monkey with me. I made that game up myself."

"You know what, Ferris, I sure wish I could go with you."

"After you got there you wouldn't have to worry about a thing. My Aunt Hallie and me do right well . . ."

"Don't you live with your mother?"

"My Mama . . . oh, my Mama's up in Chicago. She do right well too. She went away a long time ago, took the brass bed and a big yellow leghorne hat and dressed in yellow, but she send big boxes for Christmas and love and kisses."

Coin looked swiftly at his friend and heard the crying underneath the cocksure voice.

"My Mama's name is in the Bible, too, Anna Matilda Robinson. Teacher say Anna mean full of grace. Is your Mama's name in the Bible?"

"I never looked. I don't know."

They walked along in silence. Coin began to try to think of all the time he had looked in the Bible and whether he remembered the name Naomi on any page or under a picture. He remembered fifty names at once but not Naomi anywhere. Anna mean full of grace. Naomi mean . . . ? What does Naomi mean?

"I was sayin', Coin, if you got there . . . my Aunt Hallie and me do right well. We got a oriental rug on the floor. You can tell it's genuine, too, because it got ORIENTAL stamped right on the back of it.

Chinese people wove it all by hand. We got a gold chair, too, come out of the Jewish people's church. My aunt paid fifty dollars for it. Come all the way from Louisville. Come out to our house in a car. Course the gold's worn off a little. But we gonna fix that. I seen some gold paint in the Five an Ten Cent Store. Only thing we people down in Kentucky don't have that city people got is electric and gaslights and house toilets that people sit on."

"What kind of toilets have you?" Coin was thinking of all that number one and number two in the fields and everywhere.

"Wood ones out in the back yard. Our's close to the water well. Make it convenient, too."

"Who else is in your family that lives with you besides your Aunt Hallie?"

"Nobody. Sometimes my Mama send somebody down from Chicago. But they don't do nothing much but laugh with Aunt Hallie and sit on the back porch eating Concord grapes in September. Don't stay but a few weeks and then Aunt Hallie and me settle down to winter talking. Mostly about my Uncle Wayne Anthony. He's dead now. He was something, now let me tell you. He was a moonshiner of reputation. Use to go about with Reverend Talifer. Reverend Talifer was a preacher with gravy and moans. Could preach up a storm. Sometimes he'd preach a funeral and have the whole family fallin' out and nobody left to walk with the coffin but pallbearers and they'd be cryin' so hard almost drop the casket. Ever go to a funeral, Coin?"

Coin nodded his head. He didn't want to think about funerals. There would be no more funerals with him. But he couldn't help listening to Ferris. He wondered if all it was true. But it didn't matter much. He felt happy like when he was in the movies and everything happened you never saw happen in daylight and probably never could. Ferris talked on like piano music.

"In this one funeral. Mrs. Messiah from Bucket Crick. They was carryin' her to the grave singing *Now We Take This Feeble Body*. She were no more feeble. Weighed almost a ton of stones. The day was rainin' and windy. Pallbearers' white gloves filled with red mud and all. They started lowerin' the body down and got it down when one of the men's gloves slipped off and got caught in the wind. Got full of wind and puffed out and flew away like a dove. Folks got down on their knees and prayed . . . they hustled up collections and in a month hired the gravestone cutter from Louisville to carve a dove of peace to place on the grave. Folks keep it decorated with flowers. Afraid not to. And Reverend Talifer died of the shakes two weeks after. Fell into a coma callin' for Uncle Wayne Anthony's moonshine. Before he took sick he baptized me in the river. The water was cold. I trembled, boy. He wore a furlined robe. Think probally that's why he died. He had the crossed eyes. You ever drink moonshine, Coin?"

"No."

"I only did once. Tasted pretty good. Like molasses with somethin' sharp in it. Sassafras taste. Made me feel like I was risin' and fallin' and everythin' I wanted seem to come true. Felt like I was walkin' the waters and standin' on quicksand an never sink one inch. Didn't drink it but the one time. Reverend Talifer sent me out to Uncle Wayne Anthony's. You leave fifty cents on a stump in the woods and go away to drink from a cool stream an when you come back your gallon jug is full. Asked Uncle Wayne Anthony how he made it. You put your molassas barrel in the cellar and sprinkle kerosene on the inside and then light it."

"Didn't the barrel burn?"

"You sure can cut the monkey in your mind, Coin; no, it didn't burn, that made the agin' charcoal. Then you pour in your corn whiskey and let it get strong for a year. Sometimes they take it out sooner. Tasted better, they tell me. Lord, never forget Reverend Talifer moanin' before he died, moanin' that he didn't want to die and go to hell before he got to go to Chicago. Uncle Wayne Anthony went once. When he come back they said he was crazy. But I just listened to his stories. Say they got enough lights there to fairly blaze up the sky. What time you reckon it is, Coin?"

There was no time on any of the buildings they passed. Coin could see the arches of the station and the statues standing around the top. The capitol dome in the distance looked like a wedding cake. An auto honked as they raced across the clearing leading to the station and they stood stock-still while the driver laughed. Ferris poked out his tongue and muttered something.

Afterwards Coin could never quite figure how Ferris got his lunch box before the train pulled out. It all happened so fast. The conductor was yelling out "all aboard" when he remembered the melted chocolate bar he bought to give Ferris. Steam was rising from the wheels and people were running and hopping up the steep steps. Ferris was behind a dusty window with his nose pressed looking at him and waving. Suddenly Coin ran up the steps and into the hot coach. Thrusting the wet Hershey bar into Ferris' free hand he ran out to the platform again. A whistle blew and he heard the first chunk-chunks before the train started. His heart was in his mouth. Ferris was going. Coin cupped his hands suddenly and called, "What's your address?"

Ferris pointed to his ears and shook his head. Coin made out like he was writing as he called the question another time. Ferris began to write in the dust of the windowpane as the train started moving. Coin trotted by the side and as the chunk-chunks got louder, the wheels whirled faster. Coin could hardly keep up. He couldn't read a thing Ferris was writing. Something like a W but it was all backwards. No. It was an M—M—A—D—if he was cross-eyed he could read it in no time. The train was going lickety-split and he could hardly keep up with the tears running down his eyes and he couldn't see even if he could read backwards. M-A-D . . . what's the next letter? He couldn't make out if it was a C or an X or what. The last thing he remembered was Ferris' face behind letters and dust, the big eyes looking at him. The questions about Concord grapes and how far was Kentucky, where his mother's name was in the Bible, the answers were running away.

"Ferris, Ferris, Ferris, write me, write me a letter, write me . . ." He bunked into a post. When he sprang up the train was turning around the bend and he couldn't tell which coach Ferris was on.

T HE walk back seemed a trillion times longer than when he was walking with Ferris. Everything he had forgotten about like his dirty clothes, the itching in his eyes, the heat that steamed thicker and hotter with each block, the dark faces ignoring him, the other faces grinning at him, the meeting with his uncle at the Jim-Jam Cafe, all came back to him suddenly like a smack in the face and he felt like a criminal and these feelings and memory were the evidence. Then he knew what it was when he reached the park and heard the Santa Claus bell—he was lonely and the clothes, torn and dirty, the dried blood on his hands and all, were nothing compared to not knowing where Ferris lived exactly. Kentucky was big; Louisville, near Louisville. Maybe what he remembered were clues: quicksand, he'd look up all places of quicksand, there wasn't quicksand all over, and a house near Louisville with a Jewish Synagogue chair. The bell followed him ringing the name of his found and lost friend. Ferris' shining nose lighted his air and Coin sweat. Ferris was living and he would see him again with the minnows fairly blazin' and the honey in the bee ball. Uncle Troy would be willing to wander there, Uncle Troy loved him and was always willing; he would lead the way. He almost heard his uncle's stick tapping on road after road, in blue grass, in big cities, tapping like a treasure finder until they found the house. And when he caught sight of Ferris lying in the grass near the mountains like molasses puddings, he would say about his mother's name in the Bible and by that time he'd know what Naomi meant. It must be in the Bible: the prettiest name he knew. He'd say, "Ferris, here's my mother's name. Right here on this page, chapter so and so, verse so and so. I found it, Ferris, in the small print, no littler than a speck but I found it and here it is in the small print."

It was holy now in the streets with twilight and a first star. Esther would have recited.

> *Starlight, star bright,*
> *The first star I see tonight,*
> *I wish I may, I wish I might,*
> *Have the wish I wish tonight.*

Saying the poem out loud made him feel better. Somebody moved against him muttering, "Boy talking to himself. Must be a crazy boy."

Laughter sounded around him and he looked into faces and didn't see them as he moved along. He knew you mustn't tell nobody what you wished on a star but he wanted to tell everyone and if he did the wish wouldn't be reneged. Faces and faces and no one to tell. Feeling sure of what he would accomplish tonight when he got back to Mrs. Walker's, he ran through the hot twilight to find the Jim-Jam Cafe.

On the corner of Seventh and P, the Salvation Army people were playing the tambourine, and a pump organ made sour sounds and two old sisters were singing in a double-egg beater sound,

> *My faith looks up to Thee,*
> *Thou Lamb of Calvary,*
> *Savior Divine;*
> *Now hear me while I pray,*
> *Take all my . . .*

Across the street some other music banged out loud to make the Salvation Army weak. The enemy music beat drums and got louder to make the whole street listen. A singer's voice shot out,

> *If you can't can-can,*
> *Then can it,*
> *I'll buy ten dollars' worth,*
> *Say, if you can't can-can,*

> Then can it,
> I'll buy . . .

Coin continued his running. He couldn't stop to hear which side would win. Far down the street the bright sign reading JIM-JAM CAFE tilted toward him and he stopped short. Now that he was there he didn't want to go in. He recalled the last time when he had left his uncle alone for a whole day. He had had to take him home in a taxi and when they arrived at Mrs. Walker's, there was a time getting Uncle Troy into the house without raising a rumpus. That next morning Uncle Troy had cried blind tears, drinking whiskey from a half-pint bottle and feeling the pennies and nickles and dimes. He cried until he fell asleep and scattered all the money on the bed and floor. Coin had taken a blanket and covered him up because Mama always said, don't fall asleep without some cover over you or you'll catch cold. Later he found the pink gums and broken teeth near the door.

So, he was afraid to go through all that again and he didn't want to stay out late because his homework was the Bible tonight.

Laughter floated out of the open door of the café and several people were standing outside patting their feet and spitting. He never could understand why people in front of cafés spit so much. Maybe spitting whiskey out and cigarette bits. Over the entrance a woman leaned out of the window and began screaming, "Gladys, Gladys, you Gladys, bring me my back scratcher." The crowd below bellowed with laughter and there wasn't any Gladys around, let alone a back scratcher.

In the alley at the side a little man was fighting a great big tonny woman. Her hair had come loose and the front of her dress was torn showing her tiddies. Points looked like the heads of snakes, wrinkled and evil. The man had her head in a half-nelson and with his free hand he was slapping her face while she yelled toilet words. Nobody seemed to care what happened to her. Coin wanted to help but knew that would be no use. Finally the man let her free and she stumbled into the green light that came from the café windows. The man followed her and gave her a boot in the behind with his knee and she fell forward with her arms hugging the pavement in pain. Soon she sat up, rubbing her legs, muttering, "Goddammit, goddammit, look what you done to my brand new stockings."

The crowd laughed and hugged each other laughing and did jazz steps laughing as the tonny woman followed the little man into the café slapping her basketballs behind like a hurt animal stumbling to a green and smoky cave.

Looking into the café Coin saw two sad-eyed boys come out of nowhere and go over to the woman stroking her hair. In a minute the three came out and walked slowly down the street. Coin watched and determined now to go in and find his uncle and help him if he was in trouble.

He stood in the midst of a crowd between booths. A

man with a twisted face and purple lips told him to wait, he'd get his uncle. He smiled and patted Coin's head and Coin smelled whiskey around his head as the man limped away and disappeared into the door marked GENTS.

Over the bar were all the signs he had read many times before and he noticed some new ones:

WE DON'T GIVE CREDIT AND YOU AIN'T IN HELL
IF YOU WANT CREDIT, COME ON THE DAY YOU DIE
IF YOU CAN GET HERE

WE DON'T ALLOW NO DAMN CURSING HERE
THIS MEANS YOU!

IF YOU WANT TO PET YOUR GIRL
TAKE HER TO A PET SHOP

Purple Lips came limping back

"Hey boy, your uncle left a long time ago and said for you to wait here. Sit down."

He pointed to a booth where a woman with a pink derby hat slanted on her head like a strawberry ice cream scoop was sitting next to a string-bean shaped woman. Coin started over. These were his uncle's friends, he had seen them often. Purple Lips said to the string-bean woman, "Move over, Maudina. Whee, you sure do stink."

"I got the nerve to," and Maudina lifted up her arm and sniffed while Strawberry Hat shook with laughter.

Coin didn't want to slide into the crowded seat next to Maudina but Purple Lips pushed him gently and he sat down with his hands clasped before him like sitting-up-tall in school.

Strawberry Hat giggled. "Relax boy, you ain't in no school, sure ain't. We ain't gonna hurt you. Would you hurt a little boy, Maudina? Would you hurt a little boy, Jack? Would I hurt a little boy pretty as this brown dumplin' here? Hell-damn-spit no! I ain't got no hurt in me, have I, Jack? But I been hurted."

The three of them roared as if Strawberry Hat was funny as a side show in Coney Island. Coin didn't crack a smile. It was hot near mayonnaise smelly Maudina, especially after she put her skinny arm about him and kissed him until he felt her hot tongue in the roots of his hair to his scalp. He felt as though she were kissing her smell into him to last forever and began to squirm. She only held him tighter but finally took her lips away.

"Coin, Coin, penny boy, you been fightin'. You ought to have some ginger ale, if you been fightin'. Jack, go get this egg dumplin' some ginger ale, he been fightin'. His uncle will pay for it and if he won't, I will. This chitterlin' has been fightin' and he needs some ginger ale."

She pressed the sweating Coin tight and then let him go quickly.

"Jack," she said leaning on the table, "I'm sick. I'm gettin' sick to my stomach, so go get this copper penny some ginger ale."

Purple Lips limped to the bar. Maudina raised her head again and looked Coin full in the face.

"Don't mind me, honey, don't mind me. I gots a boy somewhere. I means I had a boy . . . a dumplin' . . . he run away, run away into the wilderness, into the wilderness . . . New Chicago, somewhere, Detroit, somewhere . . . that's why you gonna have your ginger ale. Maudina gonna see to that if it's the last drink she takes."

"Shut your mouth, Maudina, with all that stuff," Strawberry Hat hissed.

There was a tall glass before him with a lot of ice. Just seeing the ice made him more comfortable. He drank the whole glass down without hardly tasting a thing he was so thirsty. Maudina sputtered, "That's right, chitterlin', drink it all. Now, Jack, you see this honey's finished, you get him some more. We gots to treat Troy's boy right. Go on, Jack, my boy in the wilderness, goddammit."

Purple Lips walled his eyes at Maudina but limped back to the bar just the same.

With a second and a third drink in his stomach and ice in his mouth, Coin began to agree with Maudina, almost began to like her. But in a minute with the ginger ales and the smoke and the green light, the crossing talk, the stomping to music, the shaking floor and the mayonnaise smell, he felt like he was in a jello room. The bar kept zooping out of sight and in again. There was a singer called Gertrude who was going from booth to booth singing in a loud voice the color of the green light.

> *I'm in love and my man's*
> *Gonna welcome me,*
> *My man's gonna welcome me*
> *When I gets home tonight,*
> *Wait and see*
> *How he's gonna welcome me.*

She sang the words over and over. When she got to Coin's booth she began shaking her hips and then went to another booth with her behind grinding in the air.

Strawberry Hat leaned across the table to Maudina and at the same time put her arms around Purple Lips. The hat seemed to drip and the table tilted. Strawberry ice cream over everything, Coin thought vaguely.

Maudina yelled, "Take your arms from around my Jack."

Strawberry Hat answered louder, "I only got but one arm around him. And I takes that off this minute. I thought we was all friends but you ain't nothin' but a crocus sack, there now." Suddenly her voice got low to a whisper. "That's all right. I ain't got no boy, and I ain't got no regular man but you know what Jack and look here Maudina, I'm gonna be the first lady in Washingggtonnn to drive a Cadillac down Seventh Street in Dee Ceeee . . . I mean the first colored lady to wheel a Cadillac down Seventh Streeeeeet. You hear me Maudina, you hear me Jack, you hear me Coin."

A voice inside Coin said go home, go home, Coin, go to bed.

"And you know what else . . . and more than seven

derbys, I'm gonna have me besides this here pink one. I'm gonna have a red and a green, purple, yellow and magen . . . magen . . . what in hell's the color, Maudina . . . magenta, that's it. I love magenta. And I'll wheel down the street . . ."

Your hat's dripping, Coin wanted to say out loud but his lips couldn't frame the words. And then he saw something wiggle at the bar like a garden snake, like Uncle Troy's stick folding up in a wiggle. He began to sing the little tune about the soldier in the grass with the bullet up his ass . . . up his ass, in the grass, grass. He almost fell forward singing and he realized that there was a laughing crowd around the booth and began to sing *The Lost Chord* in alto and soprano just to show them. The words came out all mixed up and he slopped down between the women and almost wet his pants.

"This boy's drunk, I do believe. Jack, what you give this dumplin'?" Maudina's voice crashed in his ears and his head jerked up. "Jack, I say what you give this boy!"

From a long distance Coin heard Purple Lips answer, "I ordered ginger ale. I didn't pour it and I didn't taste it. How in hell do I know what this boy been drinkin'."

"You got this sonny drunk and I'm gonna take him home if I can make it. Do you know where he live?" Maudina's voice had a needle in it.

"I don't know where he live any more than you do. You ought to know, you been there with Troy often enough."

"I been there. Course I been there; who was gonna

take him home when this sonny wasn't around. Yes, I been there but I don't remember, I swear I don't remember where that blind fool live. I didn't mean that blind, I didn't mean it penny boy. I only wants to get you home and under lock and key. The world's wide open and my boy is lost. . . . Detroit or New Chicago . . . one . . . Oh, get this sonny home. I'm drunk before this sonny, drunk and I mean to drunk . . . drink some more, so take him home . . . !"

Coin heard a long snore with a whistle like a harmonica folding up in his dreams. Someone was screwing screws in his head and in his ears and he felt tight and loose and droopy. From his legs, his fingertips, down from the top of his head where the kiss was, past his eyes all things where he looked began to leak and there was a burbling zoop in his stomach. The room shot up to the ceiling and came down slowly. With his hands to his mouth he climbed over Strawberry Hat, and bumping against laughter everywhere he ran to the door marked GENTS. When he came out a million eyes were on him and he scrunched his toes in to walk straight. Mirrors at Coney Island where the skinny were fat and the fat fatter than a world balloon, people were caved in or poked out and always the blurred heads into green smoke. He thought the green smoke would choke him and he held his breath before he walked straight into the arms of Purple Lips, fell limp in them.

When he awoke everything seemed in the dark distance and as his eyes got used to that dark the familiar objects in the room came like a close-up in the movies. He looked across to Uncle Troy's bed. It was empty. In his head the soft throbbing seemed to be speaking, his mouth tasted like smell of a frog he and Abie had caught and examined long ago. Underneath him the sheets were wet from his sweat. He raised himself slowly and carefully as if he were his mother's best china and looked out onto navy-blue heat. Nothing was in his head except the idea of water. He licked his sour lips.

He decided to tiptoe downstairs and if he was quiet he would have water and food. He pulled the sheets off and headed into the darkness to the door. Softly down the first flight of steps holding onto the bannister, around the corner, past Mrs. Walker's door, down another flight, around another corner and straight into the kitchen where the icebox waited for him like a treasure chest.

When the icebox door went clip, he thought it must have awakened the whole house, so he waited a long time before he took a step as a tryout and then another. Since nobody cried out he began his getaway up the steps. Cats in the alley wailed their baby sounds but he knew them and wasn't scared. His head began to ache and there seemed to be scrinchy bits of light before him. Clinging to the bannister at the head of the steps near Mrs. Walker's door, he let himself down carefully to rest a minute. A wind blew up the stairs and the door began a slow swinging. When the wind stopped the door was half open. From Mrs. Walker's room he became aware of a springing sound and whispers and gulps; sometimes low laughter like when you were tickled and couldn't let the fun sounds out completely. He was trapped now. If he stayed he might be caught and if he ran he was sure to be.

He hardly dared to breathe when he noticed from the corners of his eyes that he could see through the opening two figures on the double bed, black against the blue square of window. As he turned his head a mosquito landed on his nose and began working there; he dared not lift a hand to slap it. The sting spread. Woody always said that when a mosquito stings you, it dies. The mosquito was dying now. Ha ha. The sounds, behind the door, brought his eyes back to the opening. If the police were chasing him now he couldn't move to save himself. Smells surrounded him. Mothballs in closets, perfume from the bureau, a close smell worse than under arms or toejam. Something knocked in his head rap rap rap. Then he heard the talking, quiet, clear.

"Lord, Troy, you ain't blind; your eyes in your fingertips," he heard Mrs. Walker say with a sneaky chuckle.

"I reckon I know my business."

"You reckon; I reckon you know mine."

"It's a long time in between times but I manage. You know, it's kinda funny, but women and girls, they seem to be afraid of somebody that can't see. Like I could practice magic on them."

"You done performed some more magic on me tonight. I mean this morning. Lord, it's most time for the dawn. Troy, you is a good man and you makes good too with them pencils and chewing gums too."

"I don't do bad. Manage to keep body and soul together."

"And that's about all most anybody can count on too. This boarding house 'bout run me crazy with no man like you help and comfort. I needs somebody to talk to."

"I knows exactly what you mean, Mrs. Walker."

"Still callin' me Mrs. when you knows my name's Clarine."

"I got lots of respect for you."

"Now that you said that, pronounce my name right."

"Clarine."

"That just about the gist of it." Mrs. Walker's voice had flowers in it.

There was a long pause. He knew now where his uncle had been while he was at the café with all the crazy. He knew now what his uncle had been doing with Mrs. Walker in the bed. The dirty thing. And they talked about it afterwards like it was nothing. He commenced to pant.

"I know what you mean, Clarine, but you see I wander. Been wandering all my life over city after city and I ain't sure I could settle."

"Moment ago you mentioned Coin. Why you bring that boy with you?"

"Sounds funny, but I wanted a little boy's hand to hold onto."

"You needs a full-fledged woman to hold onto."

"I reckon so."

"What, Troy, is you going to do when school begins. He won't be much help then."

Coin began to feel cold and hot. Mrs. Walker was hatching something to spoil looking for Ferris. She's a dirty old lady. Dirty and funky.

"Stop tickling me man, now stop. I wasn't made to be tickled."

She wasn't made for nothing. His right foot had gone to sleep. He held it out and wiggled his toes. He didn't want to cry but he felt something coming. He was lonely enough to do almost anything. Mrs. Walker's under-the-covers laughing made him mad. He was thinking so hard, trying to wake up his foot, he only caught the tail end of what they said next.

". . . why then, if you feels that way about it . . . he got a home, ain't he, and a father and all? Send him on home and get yourself together for the future. Lord know life is short. We ain't got much time. I been alone too long . . . too long, Troy. My husband died on the afternoon of the annual church picnic, in July, carrying a milk can of lemonade to the cradle roll children, and since that day I done had a makeshift heart in me. I feel like I'm about to come to the end of my rope. I need somebody bad and you the one I got to have."

"I'll think about all you say, Clarine."

"Well, let's get some sleep, I got to be up in about an hour. Let's get some sleep."

"Goodnight, Clarine."

There was silence. He'd better go as soon as the first snores.

"Clarine."

"Yes."

"I loved my sister. Didn't see her much but she were always buried somewhere in my thoughts. And Coin's her boy. I wanna do what's right."

"You better get you some sleep and think on that tomorrow but remember what I said. There ain't much time."

A long sigh. Then the cats began; one woke another up and the long wailing crying ran down the alley like a relay race. The fighting began too, so loud you'd think the night everywhere in sight would wake. This was his chance for a getaway. He stood up quickly and grabbing the bannister for support started for his room. Once he stumbled as a dog began to bark through the screaming cats. Mrs. Walker's voice shot behind him like a bullet.

"Who's that? I say who's that?"

He was in his room now behind closed doors, locked doors. Away from the secret words and the promises and the plotting about him. Away from their damn dirty. Well, he didn't want to stay anyhow. He could run away and they could all say he was in the wilderness. He'd get to Ferris. He'd leave first thing in the morning. But first there was the name. Finding that name was the only thing left for him to do. There was nobody to say goodbye to. And no one to go with him. In the school play he saw last year he remembered when someone was going on a long journey, a boy dressed in a Jesus robe came up to the traveler and said, "Everyman, I will go with thee." On the stage of P. S. 64.

The sentence stayed in his head for a long time as he stared out the window, afraid to look away from the night where it would be a morning, his morning. "Everyman, I will go with thee," he said aloud, then turned suddenly as if the words had been said behind him by another voice. Almost his mother's voice. He said the words again. He had gone with Uncle Troy but no one would go with him. Maybe, and he dug hard into his mind to make what he knew was there clear to himself, maybe he was his own everyman. Popa had said something like that before he left home. "No one can show you the way, Coin, you find that alone. Mama might have been your shield and buckler had she lived, verses from the Bible are signs but mostly you seek alone. That's growing up."

Tomorrow he would be running away. Running into trouble maybe. But his saved-up money was safe. He could eat. He could buy a ticket maybe on a bus to Louisville. That's what he'd do. Suddenly the fear came that they wouldn't sell a boy a ticket for so long a trip. An idea came. He would find the sign Agnes made for him when he was coming to Washington and print one just like it and pin it on himself. And if the ticket man said why didn't your mother buy the ticket herself, he would say that she had to go to work. She just give him the money and some lunch. He'd take the regular lunch Mrs. Walker fixed and save it to show. He went over the plan in his mind, once, twice, three times and it sounded good as the movies. He panted with excitement. If only Woody was watching. Fraidy cat up the cat's tail, he wasn't no fraidy cat, not on his life. And he would come back and face them all big as life. And ready to marry Esther, he'd come with his hands overflowing with aggies, with diamonds. He'd bring the synagogue chair back for her father to sit in. In his excitement he began to pick his nose but stopped. Ferris had told him, "Don't pick at your nose or you won't grow up to be as pretty as you think."

He'd answered, "Do you think it will ruin me."

He laughed. Turned a somersault. It was all planned and settled. If everything went okay, he'd give God a chance again. Mrs. Walker and Uncle Troy could have their old baby and have it twice. He turned another somersault just for good measure and his feet landed on the Bible Mrs. Walker had left there two weeks ago. Quietly he picked up the book and held it for a moment. His face screwed up tight as he remembered his promise to Ferris and to himself. He was a little bit scared now with the book in his hand. Not scared of the book itself but the whole adventure. The book was the caution sign at Berriman and Pitkin: the red arm with the finger pointing. He would go, he knew, there was no other place in the whole world where he could be welcome as at Ferris'. He felt, too, like when Dr. Schwartz used to fix his teeth, how he had to hold his tongue back from the drill he wanted to feel and knew how dangerous it would be to thrust his flesh against a machine. Shoot no, I'm going, he murmured and reached for a bag of peanuts.

Sprawled on the bed with the peanuts at his side and the Bible before him, Coin started the search for Naomi. This was the thickest Bible in creation. Mrs. Walker would own it. Where should he begin. There must be a trillion names scattered in it. When he was at Wesley Bible school near P. S. 64 he won a prize for knowing the books of the Bible by heart. He recalled: Genesis, Exodus, Leviticus, 1st Kings, 2nd Kings . . . Ruth, Psalms, Proverbs . . . He couldn't remember . . . Amos and Solomon . . . That wouldn't help. Anyway all the books were printed on the first page clear as day. First he decided to look at the maps and pictures. He felt a little sleepy for small print. The Land of Canaan was shaped like a cat lying sideways with his mouth open. There was a picture of a woman in pink kneeling before a king. Below it said: *Esther Pleading For Her People.* Esther, like his Esther. Esther was his Jew. What did he mean by that? Nothing bad. He loved Esther but maybe he was wrong in thinking that Esther was a Jew. He thought of Mrs. Carth and the kike and nigger words she had used. She said she hated them all but his mother made her repent by brushing confetti from her hair when the neighbors were lined up against her. Esther didn't look different from anybody else but colored people did. Everybody acted the same. He didn't want to think harder about that and decided to begin looking. Cracking peanuts with his teeth made him wide awake. He was ready to find his mother's name.

He opened the Bible at any place. He might just hit the right spot. Joshua. Chapter 10. He decided to begin reading there because he saw the heading: *The sun stands still.*

12: "Then spake Joshua to the Lord in the day when the Lord delivered up the Amorites before the children of Israel, and he said in the sight of Israel, Sun, stand thou still upon Gibeon; and thou, Moon, in the valley of Ajalon." "13: And the Sun stood still and the Moon stayed, until the people had avenged themselves upon their enemies. Is not this written in the book of Jasher? So the Sun stood in the midst of the heaven, and hasted not to go down about a whole day."

He wished he was Joshua. He would make some sure enough changes and be in Kentucky before sundown. Turning over a thick slab of pages he read down a long list of what seemed to be just names.

1 Chronicles, 25:23.

"The sixteenth to Hananiah, he, his sons, and his brethren, were twelve:"

"24: The seventeenth to Joshbekashah, his sons, and his brethren, were twelve..."

It looked like this would go on forever. He skipped.

"30: The three and twentieth to Mahazioth, he, his sons, and his brethren, were twelve..."

It was all harder than a riddle and they all had twelve. He wished he had a spy glass to make the print bigger. Maybe if he went to the end he would have more luck.

"Revelations, 18:18: And cried when they saw the smoke of her burning, saying, What city is like unto this great city!"

There were hardly any names to speak of in the next few pages but he was surprised to find so much killing and burning, so many bandits and death and battles as he went through book after book rapidly scanning with his finger all names, for Naomi. Sometimes he read when he was interested. Job had a hard time of it but Solomon reaped the gravy. He smelled perfumes with strange names and stood with Christ in the temple. His shoulder ached and his eyes strained. He was about to give up when all of a sudden on page 262 he spied the name. It rushed to him and printed itself in big letters across the page. He was so nervous he could hardly read. His pointing finger trembled. He turned the Bible over and looked away at the first light of his morning. One hand groped for the peanuts and he began reading again, cracking the shells with his teeth and spitting them out. He got a little piece of hull in his throat and coughed until his ears burned and he dropped the book. The precious page was one with the others. The name was lost because he was so greedy. It was in the chapter of Ruth, he remembered that and found the index and the page from that. In verse eight, he saw the name.

"And Naomi said, unto her two daughters in law, Go, return each to her mother's house: the Lord deal kindly with you, as ye have dealt with the dead, and with me."

He read on from there to the end. He had found the name. He had found his mother. He felt someway from the story that his own mother was really dead but more alive than ever because she lived with him.

After he read about Ruth he thought about himself. She had stood in tears. He remembered the civics class when Miss Binatree talked about people who came from far away and seeing the strange new land of steel and stone, wept to be miles from their fields and relatives.

One part of the story he read over again nine times. When Ruth said to Naomi:

"Intreat me not to leave thee: for whither thou goest, I will go; where thou lodgest, I will lodge; thy people shall be my people, and thy God my God. Where thou diest, will I die. And there will I be buried: the Lord do so to me, and more also, if ought but death part thee and me."

He studied that passage hard until he got the gist of it. Each line seemed to get clearer as the city outside the window became like twilight.

He lay down and closed his eyes and it seemed that a solemn procession of the saints and warriors, martyrs, prophets and bandits who had begotten and begotten until the earth was full with good and bad, men and women, boys and girls, some of whose names he couldn't pronounce, all these filed around him until every nook and cranny where he dreamed was bursting. Esther, pleading for her people; the gallows of Mordecai; Moses, carving laws out of solid rock, pounding the shore until the seas parted; Joshua, standing pigeon-toed when he made the sun stand still; Job, scratching his sores; Elijah, in an airplane stationed in the middle of the air; women, screaming as the earth burned to a crisp; Habakkuk; Malachi; little David, with Coin's face on, casting wild cherry pits against a giant of the world; and most of all he saw Ruth and Naomi wandering among the wheat, picking the golden leftover scraps and saying the words of together. The people disappeared, bowing, except these two. One as pretty as Esther, the other with white hair the sun shone through like she had a saint's halo, moving toward him. They came so close. Finally they walked to his eyes in a blur. Left for him to see was: Ruth 1:8 ff., in magic print.

He woke up suddenly, swallowed hard, touching his Adam's apple. In the window before him the dawn was coming up like an ember and the sun was clean in the midst of it. He stared into the sun until the glowing brightness seemed to fill the room. He closed his eyes as if to memorize the sun and the visions in his dreams. The sun that had shone on the Bible people was a different color from any that he had ever seen, the world was different too. He would describe it to Ferris and Esther when he saw them, not ever to Agnes or Woody, especially not to Miss Horwitz or Mrs. Walker, they wouldn't understand.